A DEADLY VICE

BY JACK **PROBYN**

CLIFF EDGE
PRESS

ISBN: 978-1-912628-07-0

eBook ISBN: 978-1-912628-89-6

First Edition

Visit Jack Probyn's website at
www.jackprobynbooks.com

For Jake — these stories wouldn't exist without you.

MEET JAKE TANNER

Born: 28.03.1985

Height: 6'1"

Weight: 190lbs / 86kg / 13.5 stone

Physical Description: Brown hair, close shaven beard, brown eyes, slim athletic build

Education: Upper Second Class Honours in Psychology from the University College London (UCL)

Interests: When Jake isn't protecting lives and finding those responsible for taking them, Jake enjoys motorsports — particularly F1

Family: Mother, older sister, younger brother. His father died in a car accident when Jake was fifteen

Relationship Status: Currently in a relationship with Elizabeth Tanner, and he doesn't see that changing, ever

1

Worm

DECEMBER 2008
FRIDAY

Blackness. Everywhere. His senses distorted by the sound of an engine roaring in the distance, and thick, muscular bodies bouncing either side of him like passengers in a turbulent airplane. The thin, abrasive material over his head rubbed against his face and caused the back of his skull to itch. But with his hands tied behind his back, a set of cable ties cutting into his skin, it was a sensation he was unable to relieve. The stench of dense sweat rose through his nostrils, as though the hood had been recycled from several previous abductions. Tiny

1

dust motes crawled down his throat, making him cough and gag.

No reference points. No idea where he was, nor where he was going. No one to help him. He was alone.

But there was no time to be scared, petrified, paralysed with fear.

There was no time to think or do anything.

The vehicle gradually slowed to a halt. The door beside him opened and a strong hand grabbed him by the shoulder and hauled him out of the seat. His legs scrambled for a solid surface, but only found the chilled, wintry air that had crept along the streets of Croydon in the past few weeks.

The hand released him, and as the ground came up to meet him, his body landed on gravel and dirt, a jagged stone digging into his hip.

'Up, ya sack a shit!'

This time, two pairs of hands dragged him across the uneven surface, his knees and belly catching the worst of the stones, as they grazed and ripped into his skin. After a few feet, the coarse ground made way for grass. It was wet, damp, and instantly seeped through his entire body, chilling his thighs, stomach, shoulders, and one side of his face. Without any way of propping himself up, he was forced to surrender himself to the numbing sensation that was now spreading through his body like a virus.

The cloth was yanked from his head and, in his haste, his abductor pulled out some of his hair along with it. Before he yelled in agony, all pain disappeared as his eyes adjusted to his surroundings. He was on the ground, that much was clear. A few feet from him was a large pond – big enough to drown him in – bordered by thick rows of reeds. A brilliant circle of white light reflected off the surface of the water, which was kicked up into ripples by the wind. Out the corner of his eye, he noticed he was ringed in by four men towering over him, their features masked by the shadows cast by the moonlight.

But there was no need to see their faces. He knew exactly who they were. The men they shouldn't have pissed off, but had.

'Anthony!' A shrill voice came from his left-hand side. Anthony rotated his head and saw two more individuals in front of him. One was in a similar prone position, and the other was standing, hands in pockets, his features glowing a deathly white, save for the flashing yellow of his teeth. Anthony only knew him by his self-appointed moniker, The Milkman – so named because of his ability to always deliver. Why The Milkman hadn't called himself The Postman, Anthony didn't know. And he didn't think the timing was right to find out, either. 'So glad you could join us!' The Milkman added.

'What the fuck is going on?' Anthony asked, chewing on grass and dirt.

'Let me do the talking, Anthony,' The Milkman said. He crouched beside the other man's head and clutched a handful of hair in his fingers. 'Where's my money, Zeke? Where is it?'

'We'll have it for you soon. I promise!' Zeke

3

coughed and spluttered into the ground.

The Milkman stood, pulled his right leg back, and then swung it into Zeke's face, like a professional footballer taking a penalty. The sound of bones and teeth snapping and breaking echoed around them, replaying again and again inside Anthony's head.

'Not *we,*' The Milkman said, returning to his previous position. '*You.* This is your debt, Zeke Harrison. Not Mr Sharman's over there. But soon it will be.'

Zeke babbled incoherently as he tried to protest, but the damage sustained to his mouth and jaw was too much. The Milkman whistled, and within a few seconds, the rest of his men hurried to the back of the parked-up vehicle and produced a three-by-three-foot square steel box with a large hole cut out on one side. At the sight of it, Anthony allowed himself to freeze with fear.

Screams erupted from Zeke as he wriggled and writhed on the wet grass, attempting to break his hands free from the constraints on his wrists. He was silenced with another kick to the mouth which instantly incapacitated him, and for a moment Anthony wondered whether it had knocked his business partner unconscious.

Two of The Milkman's men crouched beside Zeke and lifted his head a few inches from the grass. Another placed the box on the ground with the hole facing Zeke, and opened it on its hinge so that it split into two like a great beast opening its jaws. Then the henchman holding Zeke's head shuffled his skull into the box right up to his neck. Lastly, in one fell swoop, another slammed it shut, and the sound sent a shiver – worsened by the damp and wet of his top – through Anthony's body. He didn't know what the contraption did, nor what it was used for – whether it was for intimidation purposes only, or whether it was used for methods of torture – but something was telling him he was about to find out.

The field quickly fell silent, Zeke's screams absorbed by the box's material. He was trapped, surrounded by three hundred and sixty degrees of darkness. Anthony hadn't noticed it, but at the top of the box was a sturdy screw handle.

'Mr Sharman,' The Milkman shouted, distracting Anthony's attention from Zeke. 'This man's debt will now become yours. Seeing as the two of you are in business together, and you get to see where all my money is going, I think it makes most sense. But first I need some assurances.'

At once, the other two men raced towards him, shoved his cable ties further up his wrists, and clamped his right hand between two metal slabs. Anthony arched backwards and caught a glimpse of what was happening to him. A vice – a metal vice similar to the ones he'd used when he was in school woodwork classes during the eighties – was attached to his hand. One twist of the handle and his fingers would crush.

And then he realised. His vice contained the same handle as Zeke's.

'Holy fucking shit,' Anthony whispered, barely strong enough to speak properly.

'I designed it myself…'

'What…? How…?'

'All I want to know is where's my money?' The Milkman crouched beside him. With a flick of the wrist, all four of his men sprang into action.

Hovering over Zeke, one of them held the cube in place, while the other rotated the handle. A quarter turn, and Zeke's body shook violently, as if possessed by an evil spirit. His screams began to seep through the cube's material, muffled, distant. Yet chilling and harrowing all the same.

'When am I going to get my money, Mr Sharman?'

When Anthony didn't answer – because the sight of his friend dying in front of him was too much – the two men behind him started twisting the vice on his hand, slowly compressing the muscles and the bones and the cartilage.

Anthony let out a scream. It stopped when the tightening stopped.

'I'll–I'll–I'll make a f-f-few calls. I can get it.'

'I don't want to know how. I want to know when.'

'Next week! I can get it to you next week!'

'You have until tomorrow evening.'

One day. Twenty-four hours. One thousand four hundred and forty minutes. Eighty-six thousand and four hundred seconds. A hundred grand. Money he didn't have. Money *they* didn't have. Money they hadn't had in a while.

Fuck.

'Time to wrap up,' came the final command.

The Milkman stretched his legs and sauntered towards the car. The men behind Anthony released the vice around his hand, removed it and then left him there while the other men remained hovering over Zeke's body.

Another quarter turn.

And another.

Slowly crushing Zeke's skull. Passing the debt over to Anthony with each twist.

Anthony watched on, paralysed, powerless. There was nothing he could do for his friend as he watched him continue to scream and shake like a worm. Until—

The unmistakeable sound of bone snapping and then, immediately after, Zeke's body lay perfectly still.

2

Open Up

DECEMBER 2008
SATURDAY
Despite having lived in Croydon all his life, Temporary Detective Constable Jake Tanner had never set foot anywhere near Beddington Farmlands on the west side of the town. The area was a vast expanse of green, brown and a dull beige, littered with dense patches of overgrown grass and reeds, spotted with sporadic ponds and a tiny river, which only a few animals were able to call home. A thin blanket of frost covered everything in sight, and in the late morning light, beads of dew glistened like sequins on a dancer's dress.

The farmland's entry points had been cordoned off by lengthy pieces of white and blue tape, and a small army of uniformed police officers were stationed around the car park, quietly discussing amongst themselves the order of the day and the previous nights' football highlights. Somewhere, beyond all the growth and bushes, was a dead body.

Jake killed the engine and clambered out of his Mini Austin Cooper – his pride and joy. It was the type of car that turned heads – and not just because he looked slightly like Mr Bean in it, cramming his six-foot frame into the cockpit, legs folded against his chest. It was his dream car, and always had been ever since he was a child, from the first time he'd seen *The Italian Job*.

He rounded the back, removed his forensic gear from the boot, and dressed himself in a white plastic suit, doubling up the gloves around his fingers. Dropping the car keys into his pocket, he started towards the cordon. He signed in his attendance and shuffled through the common access path that had already been created by one of the team. It was the single route in and out of the crime scene, so that cross-contamination and forensic disturbance was kept to a minimum.

The earth was damp and muddy, and his feet slid in the plastic bootees he'd placed over his shoes. A few hundred yards – and a few slips – later, the forensic tent came into view. It was sitting at the edge of a pond, protecting the body from the elements. It wasn't raining yet, but the dense clouds overhead looked threatening. And, according to the weather report, a weekend-long downpour was scheduled. Surrounding the tent was a red and white tape, denoting the inner cordon, the part of the crime scene which contained most of the forensic evidence. A gust of wind rustled through the thin scattering of bushes that lined the water's edge like a final row of defence, and rippled its way across the surface. In front of the tape were the rest of Jake's team. Croydon CID's finest. Clouds of vapour – the colour of the frost-laden leaves – curled from their mouths and disappeared in an instant. All were his colleagues, yet none of them were close enough to be considered his friend.

Except one.

'There you are!' Temporary DC Danika Oblak said, shuffling over to him. A Slovenian woman in her late-twenties, she was Jake's closest confidant. They'd been bobbies on the beat together, and were now working with one another to achieve their dreams of becoming qualified detective constables. She was slight, considerably smaller than him, and had a certain elegance about her. Her eyes shone brightly behind her mask, and a few wisps of her jet-black hair cut across her forehead.

'Sorry I'm late,' Jake said, grateful the mask could hide his blushes.

'About time,' the senior investigating officer, DCI Payne, said with his back turned to him. Jake recognised his deep, gruff voice at once.

Jake apologised again and approached the crowd of officers. He felt their judgmental eyes boring into him. It couldn't be helped that he was late, that his newborn daughter had been up all night, that she had been coughing non-stop, that she had a fever, that both he and his wife Elizabeth were beside themselves with fear over her. But what did they care? They'd never shown him any compassion in the few months he'd been a part of the team, so why would they start now?

'What we dealing with today then, guv?' one of the team asked.

'Dead body, Martina. What do you think?'

A flock of birds burst from the tree line and scattered into the air like a cartridge from a shotgun, as if disapproving of the insensitivity of the response. Before any of them could continue, a figure emerged from the tent and wandered towards them. Beneath the anonymity of her forensic suit's hood, Karen Rossiter's fiery red hair burnt through the fabric. She was the forensic pathologist frequently assigned to the team, and one of the most competent and experienced people Jake had ever come across.

'I was waiting until you were all here,' she said, lowering her mask to reveal a lightly freckled face and colourless, chill-bitten lips. 'Got a bit of a nasty one over there, and thought you'd all love a good start to your weekend by seeing it. ID found in his pocket suggests his name is Zeke Harrison.'

Concise and to the point, she turned her back on them and, expecting them to follow, led the team inside the tent.

Lying before them amongst the overgrowth was Zeke Harrison's body, face down, his head swallowed by a giant grey cube. Unlike most dead bodies Jake had come across – of which the number was only a handful – he thought Zeke looked like he was sleeping peacefully. He often found that thinking of them alive and well usually helped him stomach the sight.

'Whassat thing?' DI Carmichael, Jake's immediate senior, asked, pointing at the box.

'From what I can gather, it looks like a giant vice – like the type you get in schools. I think, and I'm no expert in instruments of torture – although I should be after this – but it looks likes his head's been crushed.'

'I always did think Design and Technology lessons were the best ones ever. Complete waste of time. Got to piss your education up the wall by dossing about.' Carmichael's pointless words fell on deaf ears.

'When was he found?' Payne asked in an obvious attempt to keep the conversation on track, assisted by a scowl aimed at Carmichael.

'Just over an hour ago. Woman on her morning walk with the dog, as you'd expect in a place like this. Said she thought it was a drunk passed out.'

'And you checked for a pulse, right? To make sure that isn't the case?'

Karen replied by pointing at the colour of the body's skin. It was cadaverous, as white as the frost surrounding it. 'Does he look alive to you?'

Payne said nothing and waited for Karen to continue.

'I think SOCOs are looking around the area at the

moment. From what I gather they've already lifted several footprints and boot marks, and there are clothes fibres everywhere,' she explained.

'Suggesting?' Carmichael asked.

'There were a handful of people here. There's a long piece of flattened grass just a few feet from the body.' She pointed to the other side of the tent. 'The frost has preserved its shape quite nicely. Maybe there was another individual alongside our victim.' Karen bent down and placed a hand on the top of the box. 'Which one of you lucky ones gets to come with me for the post-mortem then?' She tapped the top, producing a hollow sound. 'We'll get to open this bad boy up and see what's inside.'

Jake took a slight step back, staying out of the SIO's line of fire.

But it was no use.

As soon as he heard his name mentioned, a knot formed in his stomach.

Served him right for being late.

3

The Deep End

The first thing Jake noticed when he entered the pathologist's lab was the temperature. Frozen. Colder inside than it was outside. The only saving grace was that it wasn't cold enough for him to see his own breath. The dead needed to be kept cool, but not *that* cool. Very soon, however, the bodies in the lab would reach their sell-by date and the air would be dense with putrefaction and decay, something which the formaldehyde already in the air was battling hard to combat.

Unsuccessfully.

Zeke Harrison had been transported from the crime scene with the steel box still enclosing his head. Efforts had been made to preserve the body in situ as much as possible, but with the sheer weight of the box, it wasn't entirely effective, and Jake was certain he'd heard a neck bone snap as the cadaver was lifted into the back of a van.

Currently, Zeke was lying face down on a table in the middle of the room, with a white sheet laid over him, as if it would preserve any dignity that hadn't been robbed from him when he was killed. Present in the lab was Karen, and her assistant who'd introduced himself as Steve, but whose real name was Stefan. Jake was at the back of the room, out of the way, watching from afar. Not because he didn't want to intervene, but because it was his first time visiting the mortuary, and he felt in no way prepared for what was about to happen. He'd heard horror stories passed down from the rest of the team. The smell so bad you could taste it. The sight so horrific it became ingrained in your eyes and you saw it wherever you went.

All part of the job, he told himself.

Karen snapped her fingers in the air and waved her arm in front of him. Jake blinked back to reality. She was dressed in her green scrubs, face mask pulled tightly over her mouth, and rubber gloves moulded to her hands.

'Ready to begin?' she asked him.

'As ready as I'll ever be,' Jake said quietly, a lump caught in his throat.

'There's a sick bowl,' she said, pointing to the other side of the room. 'Or, if you don't make it that far, just use the sink.'

Jake shook his head dismissively. 'I think I'll be

all right.'

'They all say that. You wouldn't believe the amount of times I've had to babysit one of your lot because they thought they could stomach it. I tell ya, the first sign of blood and some of them just' – she drew a line across her neck – 'went bye-bye.'

Jake forced a chuckle. *Please don't let me be one of them.* He wasn't sure he could live it down if he did. *Fresh meat faints at the first sign of blood.* He could hear the torrent of abuse now.

Karen moved to the other side of Zeke Harrison's body. She wrapped her fingers around the handle on top of the steel box, and with the help of Steve, started to unwind the vice. After thirty seconds of turning, they let go of the handle and opened the device, slowly revealing Zeke Harrison's broken and crushed head. A pool of thick blood flooded out of the split in the middle of the box and slowly spread around him and onto the table, pooling into the catches beneath.

'There's your cause of death,' Karen said sardonically.

Zeke Harrison's skull had been split in two, right down the middle. Blood and exploded brain matter matted his dense black hair, and large chunks of skull fell to the side. His teeth had been crushed and had fallen out of his mouth. His eyes had exploded and left two cavernous holes either side of his head. And it was barely attached to his spine, save for a few bones and muscles and pieces of cartilage keeping it in place. It was a bloody mess, and the sight of it made Jake want to vomit.

And he did.

The bile rose out of nowhere, induced by a sudden surge of nausea and a knot constricting his stomach. He retched, covered his mouth and sprinted towards the bucket, some of the contents of his stomach already spewing over his fingers. But he didn't make it that far. Fell a few feet short and emptied the rest into the sink and kept his head there, ignoring the insidious smell and Karen's laughter over his shoulder.

He'd fallen on his own sword, and now he would no doubt be the laughing stock of the office.

With the stench still hot in his nostrils, he ran the tap, washed his hands, face, mouth, and the rest of the sink, and left the acid behind to burn his throat for the rest of the day. Soon it would pass, but for now he would just have to put up with it.

'Told ya,' Karen called across the room. 'I wouldn't take it personally. This is probably one of the worst things I've seen from a body as ripe as this. So you can give yourself a pat on the back for not chucking up sooner.'

It was a minor consolation, one he'd have to milk for all it was worth. After he'd cleaned himself, he returned to the post-mortem. In the time he'd been gone, Karen had already rolled Zeke onto his back, made an incision down his chest, folded the skin over his ribs, and started removing his organs from the body, handing them to Steve as she went. Steve then shuffled to the other side of the room and weighed them, making a note of his measurements on a notepad.

Jake watched as he returned to his previous position, the knotted sensation in his stomach gradually abating as he became more accustomed to the half-dissected man in front of him.

Karen moved about the body deftly, her years of experience coming to the fore. She was standing behind Zeke Harrison's head, holding what little remained of the man's brain in her hand when she said, 'Do you want to tell him, Steve, or shall I?'

For some reason, Jake didn't think she was referring to the half-dissected carcass on her table – unless the dead had developed an exceptional ability he didn't know about.

'I think you should have the honours of this one,' Steve replied, flashing a knowing grin.

Jake looked up at her like a confused child. And he felt like one too.

Karen lifted her gaze to meet Jake's. Her eyes were squinted, and there was a hint of a smile behind her face mask.

'How long have you been with the team, Jake?' she asked.

'Since August. Why?'

'And this is your first PM since joining the team, right?'

Jake nodded.

'Well, welcome to your first initiation. You passed.'

'Excuse me?' Jake was unable to hide the shock in his voice.

'DCI Payne loves to throw you newbies in at the deep end.'

'And there I was thinking he didn't like me.'

Karen paused a fraction as she returned to her duties. 'Well, I can't speak on behalf of that, but as for this post-mortem, you're cleared to go. And when you get back, tell Payne he'll have his report by this afternoon. We shouldn't be too long here.'

4

Action List

Jake and the rest of Croydon CID were stationed around an oversized white table that occupied most of the briefing room, a small annex situated in the corner of the main office. Everyone in the team had been called in for the latest update, where they were each responsible for bringing the team up to speed with what they were working on, and any vital updates they had, so that DCI Payne could then use that as an opportunity to divvy up the tasks amongst them. The aroma of freshly-poured coffee lingered in the air like it was a permanent fixture in the room. At the head of the room was Payne, occupying centre stage, with a single notepad in front of him and a pen placed neatly next to it. Beside him was DI

Carmichael, his greasy hair shining under the fluorescent light, laptop in front of him – the only one in the office who was moving into the digital age. Around the rest of the table were the other members of the team: a couple of detective sergeants, and an even larger handful of detective constables. In the short time that Jake had been a part of Croydon CID, he'd struggled to get on the same page with everyone. Clashes in personality and a leader board of egos usually resulted in an altercation or a disagreement – most of which Jake lost out on. Not because he was a wimp, but because DCI Payne seemed to display certain loyalties to the veteran individuals within the team. Jake gathered the impression that he and Danika were the outsiders, the runts of the litter, only to be considered when all other avenues had been investigated – something that had already been demonstrated by Jake's attendance at the post-mortem.

Payne sat with his arms resting on the surface of the table, tilting on them back and forth slowly, like a metronome, preparing himself to begin. Everyone watched in high anticipation.

'Righty, guys,' he started, lifting his head from the blank page in front of him. 'As you're all aware, we're currently investigating the circumstances surrounding the death of Zeke Harrison, a good friend of mine, a person I've known for quite some years now.'

'Didn't you arrest him, sir?' DI Carmichael asked, turning to the side. The intonation in his voice suggested he already knew the answer, but was just playing along for effect, as if it were a conversation starter that had been rehearsed beforehand.

'I did actually. One of my first arrests when I was a young DS, up and coming. Got him on a drug charge, but managed to get two years off his sentence by rolling him over and having him help us out. Since then I've got to know Zeke quite well. He's done a lot of good for the local community.' Payne grabbed his pen, removed the cap and then looked up at Jake. 'DC Tanner, I know you were looking into his life, so why don't you fill us in?'

After he'd finished speaking, Payne pressed pen to paper. In the hour since Jake had returned from the post-mortem – which had comprised at least twenty minutes of abuse and banter over his bodily fluid explosion – Jake had created a victimology report on Zeke, one that looked into the victim's history: their relationships, their businesses, their financial status, their social media profiles, their friends, family, acquaintances. Everything that could be discovered, would be, although he wasn't sure what new information he might have for his boss, given how well they supposedly knew each other.

'According to the numerous news items that appear under a search result on his name, Zeke was largely considered a Good Samaritan. According to one local article on him, after his release from prison, he'd decided his experiences had changed him and it was time to make a difference. Not only to his own life, but to others' also. The article describes him as a philanthropist, campaigner and activist, and a

22

prominent figure in the local community, responsible for cleaning up some of Croydon's drug problems through his various establishments and initiatives. Many, it would seem, revere him as a hero. And when he isn't saving lives from drug addiction and the increasing threat of turf wars, he owns several businesses. Gentlemen's clubs, casinos, bars, restaurants – he owned them all.'

'Sounds like a true alterist,' Danika said after he'd finished.

'Think you mean altruist,' DS Coker added vindictively.

Coker – or Cocker, as Jake liked to refer to him outside of work and only in tight circles (namely between himself and Danika) – was one of the detectives Jake detested most. He was a bully and a narcissist. It wasn't Danika's fault English was her second language, nor was it her fault she hadn't had the time to learn all the words in the Oxford dictionary – and not through lack of trying, either. Jake was willing to bet money that Danika knew more words than him – several thousand more, in fact. Just in a different language. And that deserved more respect than she received.

'I'd argue *we're* slightly more altruistic,' Jake added. 'Defending the public, putting our lives at risk almost everyday.'

No one agreed.

'Like I said, Zeke Harrison was a good person.' Payne sighed, shook his head. 'It's always the good people who get hurt.'

Because good people get their heads crushed in giant

23

vices every day…

Noticing the sullen atmosphere, DI Carmichael intervened. 'What else are we running with, team?'

'Forensics are analysing the footstep markings found at the crime scene,' said Coker. 'Could be a while until we get anything back from that.'

'Discussions are ongoing with many of the frequent park visitors,' said DC Helen Spencer, a middle-aged woman who was the only one who'd taken an interest in either Jake or Danika. She was the resident HOLMES expert, and was responsible for inputting information into the system, creating actions, and finding connections between different pieces of evidence. She was one of the most important officers in the team, and it was Jake's unofficial task to get her onside; with any luck, she'd be able to give him the good tasks and fob off the dross to the rest of them. 'A handful of uniformed officers are still at the crime scene, speaking with anyone who may have seen something and making a note of witness statements. They'll call it in if they come across anything fruity,' she finished.

'What about CCTV?' DCI Payne asked.

'Checking it now, grabbing what I can,' DC Alfie Cram said. He was the youngest member – beating Jake by a few months – and had been there ever since he was eighteen, after completing his probationary period and his two year stint working on the streets of Croydon. Now he was in charge of monitoring and reviewing all passive data collection, which consisted mainly of CCTV, Automatic Number Plate Recognition, and mobile phone records. Investigations hinged on the evidence or lines of enquiry Alfie discovered. He was another of the team's greatest assets.

Everyone had their own parts to play, their own roles, their own unique little opportunities to shine and demonstrate their abilities. And so far, with little going for him, it looked like Jake was just happy to be there.

He needed to change that.

'Great work,' Payne said, setting the pen back on the table. 'Right now, I'm treating this as a revenge killing. Someone resurfacing from Zeke's past – someone who's got a grudge against him. Possibly from his time in prison, maybe someone he's screwed over on a deal, but I think a good starting point is finding the people he grassed on – they'll have more motive than anyone else.'

Then he divvied out the responsibilities, moving around the room, until he arrived at Jake and Danika.

Silence.

Nothing, except a brief, almost ashamed glance.

As though they weren't even there.

'We'll have another meeting this evening, but if anything urgent comes in, let me know.' DCI Payne levered his frame out of his chair and grabbed his pen and paper. As soon as he stepped away from the desk, everyone took that as their cue to leave. Everyone except Jake.

'Guv!' he called. 'I was wondering what you wanted *us* to do next.'

Payne stopped by the door, the handle

swallowed beneath his fingers. 'Oh?'

'Yeah well, I was wondering whether myself and Danika could pay a visit to Zeke's house, see if there's anything that might give an insight into what happened to him, try and ascertain what took place in the moments before he died.'

Payne's eyes moved across the room, as if searching for an approving glance from one of the other detectives.

'Sounds like a good idea, Jake,' he said finally, and then turned to DC Spencer. 'Make a note of it and add it to the action list.'

Jake was the last one out of the briefing room when his phone chimed and vibrated in his pocket. He pulled out the device and inspected the caller ID. It read THE WIFE.

'Liz, are you OK? Is everything all right?' he asked, worried. It was unlike her to call him during work.

'I need help with Maisie. My mum…she's not picking up.'

'What's wrong? Is she still coughing?'

'She's gone really cold and her cough's got worse.'

'Have you tried calling mine?'

'Not yet.'

'Give her a ring. She'll be there in minutes.'

'Why can't you come?'

Jake rolled his eyes. As if the answer wasn't obvious enough. 'Murder. Nasty one. Don't know how long I'm going to be.'

Elizabeth sighed, making no obvious attempt to hide the dismay she felt. He wanted to be there for them both – for Maisie especially – but the demands of the job were pulling him away from his family life already. It was an alien feeling, having to choose between the people he cared about or the impression he made on his team.

'Have you tried the doctor?' he asked her.

'They're probably sick of me.'

'Better they're sick of you than not hearing from you at all. Give 'em a ring, see what they suggest.'

'I don't have the car.'

'Like I said, call my mum. Don't be afraid of her – you weren't at the wedding, were you?'

'I had alcohol in me then,' Elizabeth replied.

'I'm sure she'll be fine. But let me know if anything changes, please.' He finished the call by apologising and then telling her he loved her.

As he lowered the device from his ear, he realised Danika was waiting for him by the lift doors, arms folded.

'Ready?' he asked her.

'I could ask you the same thing, Tanner. Now come on, we don't have all day.'

5

Sherlika

Danika pulled up outside Zeke Harrison's mansion in Addington, a few miles east of Croydon. The drive was quick. Ten minutes, fifteen on a bad day with traffic. That was the beauty about living and working in this small town, everything was within walking distance. But it was one of the few areas Jake had never visited. Home to a variety of wealthy entrepreneurs, politicians and ex-footballers, the wage gap between himself and the people who lived along the quiet, private streets where each house seemed to get bigger the further you drove along, was almost as wide as the gap between his respect for Danika and his respect for the rest of the team. He'd never needed a reason to drive past and gawp at the houses as he was sure many others did – the closest he'd ever come to owning a house like this was the game of Rightmove Roulette he and Elizabeth played when they were bored. Each of them had thirty seconds to find their dream property in a specific area, and they then had to rank one another's choice. It wasn't an exciting or exhilarating game, but it offered them a new aspect of hope that perhaps, one day, they'd live in a house akin to whichever one came out victorious.

Danika killed the engine and removed the keys. Jake looked over at her, watching her slender, lightly manicured fingers running through her hair. Flashing him a smile and a quick nod, she slipped out of the car and brushed her coat down. Jake joined her, the air temperature gnawing away at his fingers instantly.

The driveway, a ring of tarmac leading up to the front door, occupied a hundred feet of space from entrance to exit. But entry was blocked by a steel gate. Jake was first to the intercom. He pressed, waited.

'Yeah?' a female replied, her south London accent thick. She sounded almost unimpressed, like they'd just disturbed her from something important.

'It's the police,' Jake said. 'Would you be able to let us in, please?'

The buzzer beeped and the gates started to part. As he entered, he got a sense of what it would be like to live in a place like this, to drive in through those gates every day after a long day at the office. A sense of prestige and a sense of accomplishment for being in a position whereby he could afford one, while everyone else looked on envious, silently cursing at him as they drove past.

By the time they reached the front door it was already open, and they were greeted by a young woman – Jake placed her in her mid-twenties, slightly older than himself – dressed in a pink and purple V-neck shirt, denim trousers that flared at the bottom, and a pair of Adidas trainers. In her mouth she chewed a piece of gum voraciously. Her hair was tied into a ponytail, revealing small hooped earrings and a pink necklace, as well as one half of a butterfly tattoo on her shoulder that was visible beneath her top, with another on her forearm: MUM. For someone who obviously had money, she didn't dress or look like it.

'Morning,' Jake began. He held his warrant card in front of her and introduced himself. Danika did the same.

'Wha's this 'bout?' the woman asked.

'May we come in?'

The woman turned her back on them and led them through a door to their immediate left. The living room. Where they waited until they were offered a seat on the sofa. Jake instantly sunk into the cushion, his body surrounded by a new type of comfort, far removed from the IKEA sofa he and Elizabeth had at home.

'Would you mind telling us your name, please?' Danika asked.

'Clarissa.'

'Surname?'

'Sharman.'

'And are you living here at the moment, Miss Sharman?'

'Yeah...why?' As the number of questions increased, the fear in Clarissa's voice grew. 'Wha's gah'n on? Is it Zeke? 'As something 'appened to 'im?'

She smacked her lips together while she spoke. Jake hoped that it was due to the nerves and tension of the situation that she'd forgotten how to consume food like a normal civilised individual, rather than a bad habit she'd developed in childhood but never grown out of. Either way, as he watched and listened to her mouth move up and down loudly, he wanted to smack the gum out of her gob. It was one of his biggest pet peeves.

'What's your relationship with Zeke?' Danika asked.

Clarissa shifted uncomfortably. 'He's...he's my boyfriend. 'As something 'appened to 'im? Why ain't you tellin' me wha's gah'n on?'

Jake glanced at Danika. It was his turn to give the news. The worst part of the job. The part he hated.

As soon as he explained to her what had happened – without going into too much detail – Clarissa broke down into a flood of tears and sat there whimpering into her hands. At the sight of her distress, Danika shuffled over and embraced the woman in an attempt to console her. After she'd composed herself, Jake continued, 'Do you mind if we ask a few questions about your relationship?'

'What d'you wanna know?'

'What sort of relationship did you have? Happy? Sad?'

Sniffling and chewing loudly on the piece of gum now lodged even more firmly between her teeth she replied, 'It's complicated. He...this ain't going nowhere is it?'

'Not unless you want it to.'

'I was his beard.'

'His what?'

'His beard.' Clarissa dropped her head, played with her fingers. 'Zeke was gay, but he didn't want no one to know nothing 'bout it, 'specially considering he owns strip clubs and casinos and all that, and 'elps with the gang kids, getting them out of dealing drugs. He thought 'e should 'ave been this macho kinda guy, that they wouldn't listen to 'im if they knew he was gay. It was Anthony's idea. He said the two of us should go out so we can keep up appearances and make it look like we was togevver. Zeke wasn't too 'appy 'bout it at first, but he came round to the idea in the end.'

Jake made a note in his pocketbook. It was the first time he'd ever heard the term being used. Another addition to his personal dictionary. 'What did you get out of the arrangement?'

Clarissa lifted her head, turned it left and right, as if that was all that was needed to make her point. 'I live off Zeke and Ant's money. I get to spend what I want, do what I want. It's not the worst...'

'Who's Anthony?'

'My bruvver, and Zeke's business partner. They own all the businesses together, but Zeke's got the majority share in all of them.'

'And where is your brother now?'

'At work prob'ly. Eloquence, the club. He 'ardly leaves the place to be honest. And it's the typa place that *never* closes. The punters stay the same, the girls stay the same. Hate it.'

'Did you see him last night?'

She shook her head, wiped a tear from her eye using the back of her hand. 'Nah, I was in all night. Dunno where Zeke was neither. He don't tell me much. 'Ardly speaks to me. Makes sure I'm all right now and then, and then leaves me to it. Only interacts with me when he needs me.'

'So you don't know where he went, or where he was?'

A shake of the head.

'And you didn't think it was strange that he didn't come home?'

Another shake. 'Ain't the first time he done it. Ain't the last.' She chuckled softly to herself, drawing a memory from her mind. 'Y'know, first time I found out he was sleeping with guys in the middle of the night, I lost my shit. We got into a big argument and he left. Didn't see 'im the next day. But I dunno what came over me. I felt betrayed. I know it sounds weird, but it 'urt my feelings, y'know?'

Jake didn't know, but he sure as hell could sympathise.

'Do you know where your brother might have been?'

Clarissa scrunched her lips. 'Sorry. Ain't spoke to

'im in a while.'

Jake quickly glanced at Danika, slightly dipped his head and then turned his attention back to Clarissa. 'I think that's everything we need right now. In the next couple of hours, we'll be sending in a team to search the property, see if there's anything we can find that might give us an insight into who may have done this. Do you have any ideas?'

Clarissa looked guilty as she shook her head. 'I wish I had something, but...' She paused. The chewing stopped. 'Although...now that you mention it...'

'Yes?'

'I heard a noise last night. It was a car. A big one, four-by-four typa thing. The doors opened and as soon as I looked at the intercom, it dis'ppeared and drove off. At first I thought it was some kids pissing 'bout – they do that round 'ere. But now I ain't so sure.'

'Does your intercom record footage?'

'Yeah. Zeke was tight on security. Always had been. Never told me why, though. Guess I just thought it was because he didn't want nothing to 'appen to the 'ouse.'

Or because he was worried someone was going to abduct him and kill him.

'Do you have anywhere you can go?' Danika asked. 'Somewhere you can stay where you might feel safer?'

'Ant's. He don't live that far away. I've got a key.'

'Pack a bag and go over there after our guys have come down.' Jake reached into his pocket and produced a business card. 'If you think of anything else, or if you notice anything strange, give my number a call, and I'll be happy to help.'

Clarissa, wide-eyed and flustered, nodded as she took the card from Jake. He and Danika were halfway out of the front door when Jake turned round and asked, 'What's Eloquence's address? I think we need to pay your brother a visit.'

The car door slammed shut behind him, quickly filling the cockpit with a welcome silence. For a while Jake sat in the passenger seat, monitoring his breathing, staring out of the window. Ahead, over a hundred yards away, evidence remained of the early morning frost that had slept on the roads and the tops of cars, trees and a lamppost stationed on the opposite side of the road. It still showed no signs of clearing. Everything outside was serene, calm, and as the wind rustled past the gap he'd left in the window, he felt a gentle draught stroke his face.

He wondered whether Zeke Harrison had felt the cold when he was pinned to the ground and crushed beneath the vice, or whether the adrenaline of imminent death had warmed him, a subtle consolation to what Jake could only imagine was a terrifying ordeal. He didn't think it likely.

The other car door shut, distracting him from his thoughts. Danika switched the engine on, and he was immediately slapped round the face by a blast of hot air pouring from the vents. Left and right, in a two-pronged attack. The stuffy air climbed down his throat and stayed there like a bad layer of mucus.

'What do you make of that then?' Danika asked as she made herself comfortable.

'That this is more serious than the guv is making out. I don't think Zeke Harrison is the hero everyone thinks he is.'

'Watch where you step, Jake,' she said, sounding like a worried mother. It was the first time he'd ever come across her maternal side. She was only a few years his senior, but already had one more child than him. 'I'm sure the guv's got a method to his madness.'

If he does I'd like to know what it is.

Jake turned his head and looked out of the window. Two halves of a wooden stick, split in half from the fatal fall from above, rolled listlessly in the wind. There were times when Jake felt like that stick, allowing the wind to carry him and move him about; and there were other times when he wanted to be the wind, to be the one to move things along.

Something about Zeke Harrison's death concerned him, and right now he didn't know what it was.

'You look troubled,' Danika noted.

Jake smirked, turned to face her, his cheeks tingling with heat. 'You should be a detective, you know that? Female version of Sherlock Holmes.' He paused, scratched the underside of his chin. 'Sherlock Oblak. Danika Holmes. Or maybe even Sherlika Obles.'

Without looking at him, she expertly shifted the car into gear while giving him the middle finger. Not the first time, and definitely not the last.

'You don't even want to know the name I have for you. In Slovenia we have a particular word.'

'I'm intrigued now.'

'Piss me off some more, and you'll find out. And before you ask, it isn't a good word.'

'No shit, Sherlika.'

6

First of Many

The person Jake was most eager to see when they returned to the station – something which even he was surprised at – was DC Alfie Cram. The scrawny, almost pre-pubescent-looking twenty-three-year-old was one of the officers who'd shown Jake the least attention since the start of his tenure. Not because he possessed any dislike or malice towards Jake, but because he was so engrossed in everything he did, he seldom focused on anything – or anyone – else. Seated at his desk, straight against the back of his chair, eyes honed in on the screen, with a pair of headphones propped over his ears, Alfie was able to block out the rest of the hubbub of the office, and by extension the entire world. Although it came at a cost. Many in the office, including Jake in an attempt to fit in and build relationships, joked about the likelihood that Alfie would find himself riddled with mobility issues later on in life, least of which would be deep vein thrombosis. During an investigation a few weeks into Jake's time at Croydon CID, where a young girl had been reported missing, the team had worked flat out for two days straight. Jake and the rest of the team were up and down, visiting witnesses, speaking with suspects, moving their legs and keeping their bodies active, whereas Alfie had remained in almost the same position for nearly forty-eight hours, stopping only for toilet and drinks breaks. Jake had assigned him an apt nickname: The Machine.

Jake approached Alfie cautiously, trying to announce his presence as much as possible, lest he shock The Machine into making a mistake or, worse, a rash movement. He moved in from the side, waving, hoping it registered in Alfie's peripheries.

It worked.

The young man removed the headphones from his head and wrapped them around his neck, the black wire dangling down his chest.

'Afternoon, mate,' Jake said, putting on a friendly face. 'You good?'

'Fine. Did you need something?'

A cold response, sooner than Jake was expecting.

'You're the man with a keen eye, right?' Jake asked, preparing himself to swallow his pride.

'Is that what they told you?'

Jake ignored the comment. Fuck it. There was no

point trying to be nice. It wasn't going to get him very far, evidently. Going against his nature and everything he'd been raised to be, he continued, 'I think we might have something for you. Myself and Danika spoke with Zeke Harrison's girlfriend, Clarissa. She said that she'd noticed a strange vehicle hovering outside the house in the past couple of weeks. They've got an intercom system with access to video recordings. I wondered if you'd be able to have a look at it?'

Alfie's face remained impassive. No hint of emotion. No hint of excitement that they had a lead. No hint of surprise that Jake had managed to exceed his seemingly low expectations of him. Nothing. *Maybe the computer screen's numbed his facial expressions.*

'Have you spoken with Helen? Exhibits? Have they raised it as an action on HOLMES?'

Have your balls grown bigger? Have you decided to rise higher than your station?

'Not yet...'

If there was one thing he hated more than being patronised, it was being belittled.

'Probably best you do that before coming over and interrupting me.' Alfie turned his attention back to the screen, placed his headphones over his ears and continued searching through CCTV footage on his computer.

A sudden urge to grab one of the cushioned earpads and snap it back against Alfie's head rushed over Jake, but he suppressed it. Some battles were worth fighting. This one wasn't.

Slightly aggrieved, but realising he was in the wrong for not following the appropriate procedure, Jake made his way to DC Spencer on the other side of the office, where he found her shovelling a handful of Maltesers into her mouth, with a can of Diet Coke in the other hand. Yin and yang. A perfectly balanced diet.

She greeted him with a facetious smile, one you might give a child after they've distracted you and have to pretend you're happy to see them.

'Couldn't get you to add this to the actions list, could I?' Jake handed her a piece of paper with instructions on it. No niceties, in and out. It might not be doing him any favours, but he'd quickly learned there was little point trying anymore.

You can lead a horse to water…

'Sure, no problem. I'll add it to the pile,' Helen told him, and placed the document on top of her in-tray.

With that, it was done, and Jake returned to his desk. Time to turn his focus away from Alfie and Helen, and instead narrow it on what mattered: finding the person, or people, responsible for Zeke Harrison's murder. He was at his desk for less than five minutes when an idea popped into his head, like a seed germinating in fresh soil. He ran with it to DCI Payne's office, a small enclave buried in the corner of the incident room. He knocked and entered as soon as he was granted permission.

The office was small, barely large enough for the desk and chair and tenant that occupied it. Jake was aware the resources in the department were scant, but he didn't know they were that thin. The obligatory picture frame containing Payne's wife and kids was resting beside the computer monitor, turned away slightly, as if to shield them from view of what he got up to behind the desk. A coffee mug, covered in stains, sat beside the frame, and was the only other item on the desk. Perhaps the budget didn't extend to an in-tray, Jake supposed. Over Payne's right shoulder, propped on a filing cabinet, was a stereo. "Sex on Fire", by the Kings of Leon, played quietly in the background.

'How can I help, Jake?' Payne asked.

Jake quickly brought him up to speed on Clarissa, Zeke's house, and the intercom footage. When he finished, he scratched the side of his chin – a natural reflex he'd developed after scarring it as a child – and shifted his weight from one foot to the other.

'Gay, you say?'

'Excuse me?'

'Zeke. Gay. You said his girlfriend was a *beard*?'

'Apparently, yes. It was her brother's decision. Anthony Sharman. Which is why I wanted to see you, sir. I think someone should speak with him. See what his movements were last night.'

'You think he's got something to do with this?' Payne knotted his fingers together and eased back in his chair, like a relaxed Bond villain.

'If the motive's anything to do with his time in prison or the gangs he's been working with, then it only makes sense that the person who spends the most time with him should be questioned on it. Not to mention Anthony's got a minority share in the businesses... Maybe he wanted Zeke out.'

Payne gave a slight nod, almost imperceptible, as though he were ashamed to show the assent and appreciation of Jake's discovery. 'That's a long-winded way of saying yes, Jake. But nice thinking.' The pain in his voice was obvious. 'Take Danika with you. Nothing like learning on the job.'

I've already done enough of that today, I think.

Jake left Payne's office feeling like he'd won a minor victory. Hopefully, it would be the first of many.

7

Unbearable

Anthony Sharman was an ostentatious little man, unafraid to use his status and wealth to impress. At thirty-nine, his hair was grey, lined with thin streaks of black. Tanned, leathery skin hugged his body and looked as though he'd spent several hours longer than prescribed on a sun bed. And he was no stranger to living a life of luxury and materialism. The Mercedes car keys sitting on his desk. The thin diamond necklace dangling from his neck, briefly on show through his Hugo Boss shirt. The Rolex watch on his left wrist. From first impressions alone – and Jake would be lying if he said he hadn't judged the man immediately – Anthony Sharman was a poser, a flash wanker.

'We're very sorry to have to tell you this, but Mr Harrison was murdered between late last night and the early hours of this morning,' Danika explained as soon as they seated themselves opposite Anthony. 'We can't go into too much detail right now, but we wanted to ask a few questions, if that's OK?'

At the news his business partner and friend had been murdered, Anthony's reaction took Jake by surprise. Sitting there, staring at them both, as if to say, "What do you want me to do about it?" There had been no outcry, no gasp, no subtle exhalation of air from the nose. Nothing. As if he'd already heard the news from elsewhere.

Or worse, known about it before anyone else did.

'Horrible,' Anthony said flatly, after a prolonged silence. 'Simply horrible.'

Anthony's office was a squalid, poorly lit room that was barely large enough for the three of them. His desk was in the middle, and behind him was a small kitchen area, complete with sink, fridge and microwave – the perfect place to hide out from an aggrieved partner or murderer. Jake didn't see any sign of a bathroom, so he wondered whether the sink was multifunctional.

'How long have you known Mr Harrison?' he asked, already making notes in his pocketbook. 'Have his family been informed?'

'Yes, Mr Sharman, they—'

'Anthony, please. Or Ant. Whichever. I'm easy-going.'

Oh good, I was worried you wouldn't be.

Jake cleared his throat and gripped his

45

pocketbook tighter in his hand as he shuffled in his seat, his trousers rubbing against the faux leather.

'I can't believe it,' Anthony continued. 'I'm just in a little bit of shock. Wow. He's gone. Just like that. I only saw him yesterday.'

'When was the last time you saw him precisely?'

'About seven. Before I went for dinner with a friend.'

'What's the name of the friend?'

'Sandra Gerringham. We went to Wetherspoons just for a drink and a catch up. Her choice. She's an old friend. From way back.'

'Which was it? A drink or dinner?'

'Both. We had a drink, and then we got some food. The two aren't mutually exclusive.'

Jake ignored the jibe. 'Can you remember what you ordered?'

'Some spicy chicken wings. And Sandra had a pizza. It's not the best food in there but the drinks are cheap and strong.'

Jake was immediately suspicious, and he made a note to check that out later. If Anthony was lying to them, they'd find out with a quick call to the restaurant followed by a check of their records – both digital and analogue.

'How long have you known Mr Harrison, Anthony?' Danika asked, moving the conversation along.

'Nearly twenty-five years,' Anthony said with an air of defiance, like his position in society was infinitely heightened by his answer. 'We met in school. Turned out we lived on the same estate. Just a few doors from each other. You could say we became best friends, and you'd probably be right. But when Zeke got done for that whole drugs thing... I didn't speak to him until he got out.'

'And how did the two of you end up going into business together?'

Anthony scratched the side of his mouth, as if wiping away a piece of leftover chicken wings. 'Zeke reached out to me a couple of months after he got out of the joint. Said he had some good ideas he wanted to share with me, ways he could turn his life around. At first I was dubious – a boy like him has enemies I didn't want to get involved with. But then I started seeing the work he was doing with his campaigns. He was making a change in the local community and I thought it would be stupid not to get involved. It covered a great PR angle.'

'Is that why you told your sister to pretend to be his girlfriend, even though he was gay?' Jake asked.

If Anthony heard the question, he showed no sign of acknowledging it. Instead, he continued, heedless: 'I had some money saved up, and he had a couple of grand that hadn't been seized by your lot, so we decided to get the ball rolling. I'm more business-minded whereas Zeke was definitely more creative. He had all the ideas.'

'Did that ever cause any disagreements between you two? Any friction, hostility?'

Anthony's face remained still as he tried to calculate an answer to the probing question. They were beginning to rub him up the wrong way. And soon enough they'd tear through the façade of cheap bling, designer suits and misguided male dominance, and get to the juicy stuff they needed.

'Every business has arguments,' Anthony replied. 'Like a good marriage. You grow from them, build from them, develop.'

'Until eventually one day you've had enough of them…and snap…' Danika said softly.

Her intrusion took Jake by surprise. It was no secret between the two of them that she was going through relationship issues of her own – she usually used him as a sounding board to help her keep things in perspective – but she made a strict habit of keeping such things separate from her professional career. Except, on the odd occasion, like this, where the two melted into one.

'You said so yourself,' she continued after realising the tense atmosphere she'd caused, 'a man like Zeke has enemies. Were you one of them?'

Anthony folded his arms across his chest, unperturbed by the insinuation. As he did so, his sleeve rolled up his right arm, revealing a golden bracelet. But that wasn't the thing that attracted Jake's attention to Anthony's wrist: it was the man's hand. His fingers and veins were a deep shade of blue, dotted with blotches of black and yellow, as if they'd been dragged from the depths of the ocean.

'Nasty bruise.' Jake nodded at Anthony's wound. 'How'd you get that?'

Anthony pulled his sleeve over his wrist. 'Shut it in a car door by accident.'

'You did?'

'No. Someone else did. My nephew.'

'Clarissa's son?'

'You've spoken to her?'

'Only briefly.'

'Well then, you'll know that she doesn't have any children. No, it was my other sister. Anna. Her boy, James. I was...I was helping him get out of the car, reached back inside and then he shut it on me.'

'When was this?' Jake scribbled as Anthony spoke.

'The other day. Can't remember exactly when.'

'You go to the hospital?'

'For this? It's nothing. Just a bruise. It'll go away soon.' Anthony's phone chimed on the desk. He picked it up and stared at the screen. Jake observed the minutiae of Anthony's face – looking for the tiniest change in expression, a hint that something was awry. There was nothing. 'Forgive me, detectives, but we're going to have to wrap this up fairly soon. I have a business meeting with one of our suppliers. And I fear I'm going to have to speak to our investors as well regarding...well, what we've discussed. Is there anything else I can do to help?'

'We'd like to take a look around, if it's all the same with you,' Jake said, already lifting himself out of his chair. 'Maybe we could speak to some of the workers around here, see what they have to say about Mr Harrison.'

Anthony tilted his head to the side. 'Why's that necessary?'

'So we can do our jobs properly.'

Anthony rubbed his bruised hand. 'Speak to Arabella downstairs, tall, blonde woman. Best in the

49

club, and she was Zeke's favourite. They were always spending time together. She's your best port of call. Oh, and there's no point talking to any of the foreign girls on the dance floors. We've got a lot of them, but they don't talk much English, and they hardly ever spent any time with Zeke.'

Anthony allowed himself to release all the pent-up frustration and stress as soon as the door closed. The deep exhalation of air from his lungs lasted an eternity. His shoulders relaxed, and he felt his mind open a little, creating a small hole of freedom and clear thinking amidst the chasm of chaos.

The deadline was looming.

Twelve hours, to be exact. And he still wasn't a hundred grand richer. Nor did he think he would be with the police breathing down his neck.

A hundred grand was a lot of money – a lot of money he didn't have. Zeke had made sure of that, keeping him abreast of the finances where it mattered, and away from all the secrets and hidden deals. They were deep in shit, and even deeper in debt.

But Anthony was by no means an idiot. He knew on a subconscious level – had *always* known – what Zeke was up to, what he'd been up to in the past few months. The sudden influx of girls working for them. The sudden influx of customers. The two new additions they'd made to their business portfolio, the casino and the restaurant, and the drug money that was being laundered through them. The corruption wheel was turning, and Anthony was going right along with it. Whether he liked it or not.

To become a part of the solution, you first had to admit you were part of the problem.

And admitting he had a problem was one thing Anthony had never succeeded at.

He listed forward on his chair and rested his arms against the edge of his desk. In front of him, on the computer screen, were several moving images from the CCTV cameras stationed around the club downstairs. His eyes searched for the officious little prick and obnoxious – but surprisingly good-looking – woman who threatened to dismantle everything he and Zeke had worked so hard for. But he came up short. There was no sign of them.

Maybe they weren't so interested in speaking with the girls after all.

He hoped.

Before he could think on it some more, he dropped his head and closed his eyes. He assessed the options available to him, of which there were only a few.

Run.

Hide.

Kill The Milkman.

All of which would undoubtedly result in his very own steel box of death.

What was he thinking, killing someone? The closest he'd ever got to ending another person's life was supplying their weak heart with too much cocaine. And even then they'd survived. He was no natural born killer. But he was no saint either.

His eyes moved away from the computer screen and fell on his mobile. The brand-new Sony Ericsson Xperia 1. A smartphone, it was called. Said to be the hottest model on the market. A new generation in technology and mobile phones. It probably had all the bells and whistles, but for Anthony it was the most expensive mobile he'd ever bought at just shy of £800. All because Zeke had thought it would be a good idea. But it had turned out to be one of the worst buying decisions he'd ever made. Good thing it wasn't his money paying for it.

Anthony picked up the device, prodded his fingers on the screen and found The Milkman's number. He dialled. He didn't expect an answer; The Milkman frequently changed his mobile number, and it was hit or miss whether the call would connect.

Fortunately, on this occasion, it did.

'You have my money?'

No, but I have an £800 phone you can take off my hands.

Anthony clenched and unclenched his fist several times. 'I don't…not right now. I'm working on it. But I need more time.'

'That's not how it works.'

'Please. I've got the police breathing down my neck. I've just had a visit from them.'

'And that's my problem?'

Anthony sighed, massaged his forehead. 'Please. Another day, at least. I'll work something out. I need to make sure the police don't find out anything they shouldn't.'

There was a silence. A long one. Anthony pulled the phone away from his head and checked the call was still connected.

'Twenty-four hours. And if I don't have my money by then, I'll make life unbearable for you.'

8

Foreign

Jake wasn't sure whether Anthony Sharman was dumb or just stupid. But then he realised they were both the same thing.

There's no point talking to any of the foreign girls on the dance floors.

Feeling like a disobedient child who didn't listen to orders, that was exactly what he was going to do. If there wasn't anything suspicious about Anthony before, then there certainly was now.

'He's got something to hide. The only question is what,' he said to Danika as they left Sharman's office and headed down a set of dark steps, lit only by a long, thin tube overhead. Plastered on the walls either side of him were posters of scantily clad women standing on podiums in provocative positions, highlighting particular events in the calendar. Jake paid them little attention.

As they descended the steps, every part of his body reverberated and pulsed in tandem with the heavy, repetitive din coming from the stereo speakers buried deep in the walls and ceilings of the club. It was a little after one in the afternoon, and the gentlemen's club was busy. At least, judging from the numbers on the floor, Jake assumed it to be busy; he'd only ever set foot in one during his stag do in Amsterdam with his university friends. Images of the women in the infamous Red Light District, standing there, dancing in the windows, waving, earning their keep, were still painfully ingrained in his memory.

The sight in front of him was no different. Ten poles, shining in the neon purple light. Strategically positioned throughout the club for efficiency – the distance between them was large enough for free movement, and a wide berth was given to the sofas and seats surrounding the poles. Five girls, wearing nothing but underwear, were currently working, dancing, swinging, wrapping their legs and arms and hair around the pole, finding themselves in positions Jake had only ever seen in the Kama Sutra book his older sister had bought for him as a joke on his eighteenth birthday. Two girls wandered about the floor, attending the patrons, catering to their every need – and receiving a generous tip for it in the process – while others stood behind the bar serving drinks. On the opposite side of the club were two red curtains, glowing beneath a demonic light, giving the room its apt name The Red Room. Standing either side of the curtain's entrance were two burly, impassive security guards, arms folded, menace spray-painted across their faces. Jake assumed it was the place for lap dances and happy endings.

'Who do we 'ave 'ere?' asked one of the women holding a metal tray of drinks in one hand while her other gently massaged Jake's bicep. 'You're tense. We 'ave the perfect thing for that.' She spoke in an English accent. Northern. Far away from home. Although anywhere would be far away from home when you worked in a place like this, Jake felt.

'I'm fine, thanks.' He brushed her aside as politely as he could. Keeping his eyes focused on hers – and not allowing them to wander down her slim, supple body – he took a step back. 'Where's Arabella? We'd like to speak with her.'

'She's working, sweetheart.' The girl flashed a set of incandescent white teeth, glowing faintly purple beneath the light. 'I'm sure I can help you in the same way she can.' She finished the flirtation with a casual wink.

Danika stepped in, waved her warrant card in the girl's face. At the sight of it the club worker retreated and brought the tray into her chest in an attempt to cover her cleavage. A little too late, but he admired her commitment to save some self-respect.

'Please…wait here.' Her voice had lost all personality as she hurried off to the other side of the club and disappeared through the curtains.

56

Jake watched her go, and as soon as she was gone, he settled his gaze on Danika. She scowled at him, unimpressed. 'You can wipe that smile off your face,' she told him. 'It's her *job* to give you attention.'

Jake didn't even know he'd been smiling. It was an involuntary reaction, a facial spasm completely out of his control. Wasn't he allowed to appreciate a little attention, even if she was paid to give it to him?

The club worker returned a minute later with Arabella hurrying after her. The girl had changed and they were both dressed in light red satin robes that covered their entire bodies. Arabella was a few inches taller than the other girl, and her long blonde hair flowed behind her like a parachute caught in the wind.

'Detec'ives...' she began, extending her hand. Her grip was strong, powerful, years' worth of pole dancing hiding behind her muscles.

Jake and Danika thanked the club worker for her assistance, and Arabella quickly led them to somewhere private, away from the noise and the distraction. To the back of the building, in what looked like a dressing room. Thick mirrors, bordered by oversized orange light bulbs, hung from the wall. Make-up wipes, brushes, eyeliner wands and nail varnish bottles adorned the surfaces, making it look like there'd been an explosion in a Boots store. The atmosphere in the room was stale, a potent combination of overused perfume and sweat – and so far the perfume was having a hard time doing its job.

'We'd like to ask you some questions about Zeke

57

Harrison, if that's OK?' Danika asked, going straight for the jugular.

'Is he…is he all right?'

'He was murdered last night. We need to ascertain what sort of man he was and who might want to do this to him.'

Out of all the people they'd informed so far, Arabella's reaction was the most visceral. Her hand flew to her mouth, tears formed almost immediately in her eyes, and her fingers trembled with shock. From the brief lecture Jake had studied on this type of behaviour at university, he deemed it to be genuine.

'When was the last time you saw Mr Harrison?' Danika continued.

'The day before last,' Arabella whimpered. 'I din't see him at all yesterday.'

'Where were you?'

'Workin'.'

'When did your shift finish?'

'Five this morning. I started midday yesterday.'

'And you're here already?' Jake stepped in.

'I started early, innit. Always do. Got nuffin' better to do at home, so might as well come in. Make some extra money.' Arabella's voice was noticeably common. She spoke with a thick, east London accent, but it sounded as though she were trying hard to mask it and cover it with something else. There were still some signs of slippage that would never disappear.

'What sort of relationship did you have with Mr Harrison?' Danika checked her watch and then scribbled the time in her pocketbook.

Without warning, Arabella turned taciturn. She eyed the pocketbook heavily, and then her eyes bounced between Jake and Danika.

'I ain't under arrest, am I? I'm not a suspect?'

'Should you be?' Jake asked, placing his hands in his pockets.

'No! God no! I was just...' She sighed. 'Zeke and I were friends. Good friends. We spent a lot of time together. Mostly at work, y'know. When I came in early, I'd spend most of the time upstairs in the office wiv 'im. Anthony didn't like it much, nor did his girlfriend, but...' She sighed again. 'I s'pose this is the time to get stuff out in the open, in't it?'

Jake and Danika nodded simultaneously without needing to look at one another.

'Well...it's funny, in't it? I spent so much time wiv 'im, and now I feel like I didn't even know 'im.' Her dialect came flooding through now.

'How so?' Jake asked.

'Well, I can't fink of anyone who'd wanta do this to 'im, y'know? I always thought 'e was such a lovely guy. Kind, sweet, caring. But...some'imes there was this darker side to 'im as well.'

'What do you mean?'

'He had the tendency to snap, y'know? On some level, I think ev'ryone does. But when he got angry, he got *real* angry.'

'What did he do?' As he waited for a response, Jake's eyes wandered around the room. At the hair extensions draped over the backs of the chairs. At the bottles of talcum powder and packs of chewing gum on the surfaces. At the foreign imported cigarettes and tobacco pouches beside them.

'He'd just lose his temper and scream at people. He never hit no one, though. It was…it was just a darker side I din't like.'

'What did he get angry over?'

'He never told me no specifics. Fings goin' on outside all this, I fink. If people wasn't gettin' paid. If people wasn't payin' him. Kept talking 'bout not havin' enough money to make payments they needed to.'

'The company was under financial pressure?'

Arabella shrugged. 'I dunno for definite.'

Jake's eyes fell on a small, transparent plastic packet sitting amid the detritus. Tiny specks of white powder remained in the corners, and it looked as though its user had been in a hurry to use it.

He looked at Arabella. 'Did Zeke ever take any drugs?'

'God, no. Never. Ever since he done his time for it, he was tryna get people off 'em. You musta seen that in the news.'

Jake nodded. 'Did he ever sell it to you or any of the girls?'

Arabella shook her head vehemently. 'He din't deal with none of that. Tried to keep as far away from it as possible.'

Jake nodded his assent, looked at Danika and then nodded at her.

'One more question before we go,' Jake started. 'We'd like to speak with some of the other girls here… Where are they?'

'They're all out the front.'

'Not those ones. The "foreign" ones.' Jake used his fingers in air quotes.

'I, erm…they're…they're through that door over there.'

'Why are they separated from the rest of you?'

Arabella shrugged. 'Zeke always said it was cos people have different tastes 'n' that. Not everyone wants a British girl. Some blokes find the other girls more exotic, and they liked them all separated, so we had ta give the punters what they want.'

Jake and Danika thanked her for her time, gave her a business card with their details on, and headed through another door at the opposite end of the room. Above the door was a sign that read "Pink Room", denoting the name of the place they'd just entered, as if the luminous pink lightbulbs surrounding the frame weren't an obvious enough indicator.

The Pink Room's dressing room was similar in terms of shape, size, layout, and the disorganised mess on the tables. A single woman wearing matching underwear, hair dangling off her shoulders, was sitting on the chair with her back to them, fiddling nervously with a tobacco packet.

Danika cleared her throat.

The woman flinched and threw the tobacco onto the desk in a fashion that made Jake wonder what else was inside it.

'Easy! Easy!' Danika said, hands raised in defence, moving slowly towards her. 'We're the police.' She reached into her pocket and produced her warrant card to demonstrate they meant her no ill will.

The woman leapt out of the chair, retreated from them, panicked, and suddenly started speaking in Slovenian, her lips moving rapidly, eyes moving faster than her mouth.

Then Danika spoke, and as soon as the club worker heard her native language, she stopped.

Jake realised it wasn't his place and so took a step back to let Danika handle the situation herself. There was nothing more that he could do – he didn't have the ability to instantly learn a new language, and Google Translate wasn't that far developed, so he'd have to sit this one out.

After a few minutes of discussion, Danika thanked the woman, handed her another card, and let her leave.

'Good, bad, ugly?' Jake asked. 'And I'm not referring to her appearance.'

'She was frightened,' Danika said. 'You saw the way she was – as soon as she saw us, she freaked.'

'She say anything important?'

'Not exactly…' Danika placed her hands on her hips.

'What you thinking, Sherlika?'

'I think she's being exploited. I think she was trafficked into the country. Along with all the other "foreign" girls.'

9

Scarce Resources

'Sex trafficking?'

'That's right,' Jake replied.

'Human trafficking...slavery...'

'All of the above, guv,' Jake said to DCI Payne. For a man who had spent the bulk of his thirty year-long career as one of the highest-ranked officers in the Met – and was supposedly a very intelligent man – Payne seemed to be having a hard time grasping a simple concept.

He stood there with his hands on his hips, an expression of discontent drawn across his face.

'I find it difficult to believe Zeke would be involved in that sort of stuff. After all the good he's done. What's your source?'

Danika stepped in. 'One of the club workers, guv. She's Slovenian. She told me that she and the rest of the girls were scared.'

'But she didn't tell you about what...'

Danika's gaze dropped to the floor and she took a step back.

The three of them were in the briefing room, Jake and Danika at the opposite end of the table to Payne. Sometimes Payne enjoyed spending time in there. It was quiet, and away from the madness of the investigations. Not to mention the space was bigger. His theory was that, if he was going to make decisive actions, he needed to be in the right mindset for it. Jake hoped he was calm enough to make one of those choices now.

Payne turned away and shuffled towards the wall. In the middle of one of the whiteboards was a printout of Zeke Harrison's face.

'That his mugshot from when you arrested him, sir?' Jake asked in the hope that his attempt at massaging his boss's ego would work in his favour.

'Yeah. Poor fella looked so young back in the day.' Payne paced to either side of the whiteboard, shaking his head. 'I just can't imagine it. Since Zeke got out of prison and started his youth clubs and the clubs of his own, I've never seen anything to suggest that he and his associates might be capable of bringing in Eastern European women for work.'

'You know what they say, guv.'

'Whassat?'

'It's the ones we least expect to hurt us that eventually do.'

Payne stopped, placed his hands on the back of his chair. 'Think you might be in the wrong career, Tanner.'

Jake shrugged. 'Just helps to know how people's minds work. Zeke's murder is unusual, guv. The method in particular. It looks carefully organised. And there was definitely more than one person present. I think Anthony Sharman, Zeke's business partner and friend is a significant person of interest. When we spoke with him, he said that he was out for a meal at the local Wetherspoons on the night of Zeke's death. I checked it out, and it was a load of BS. There was no evidence he was ever there, and to be honest, he doesn't look like the type that'd dine at a place like that. He also lied about who he was with. And he had a bruise on his hand – looked as though it had been badly crushed by something. He said it was his nephew shutting it in the door, but as far as I've been able to make out, he's only got one sister. And she only found out this morning that her gay boyfriend is dead.'

'The man's got something to hide.'

Jake nodded. Finally, getting somewhere. 'What about—?'

He was interrupted by Payne's mobile ringing. The DCI held a finger in the air, placating Jake, and then answered the call, moving closer to the corner of the room so he was just out of earshot.

He returned his focus to them thirty seconds later.

'Uniform have just arrived at Harrison's gaff to search the property,' he said. 'Something you should have done when you were there. Guess what they've found...'

'Another fake girlfriend?' Danika asked behind Jake's shoulder.

'Drugs. A whole shipment of them. Mostly weed and coke. Kilograms of the stuff.'

The news was bittersweet. Yes, it meant that Zeke's secrets were all beginning to unravel, but on the other hand, it was something Jake and Danika should have investigated when they were there, speaking with Clarissa. They should have been more thorough and proactive. They were lucky the drugs were still there. If Clarissa had been involved, or if anyone else who knew about them had found out that Jake and Danika had visited the mansion, then there was a high possibility those drugs could have found themselves halfway across the country by now.

Luck, and time, for the most part, were on their side.

'Maybe our community hero wasn't so much of a hero after all,' Jake added disparagingly.

Payne stopped tapping his chair and placed one hand on his hip, while the other pointed to the other side of the room. His nickname around the office was Teapot – not because he liked tea, but because of the way he stood.

'I want you two to look into drug dealers in the area,' Payne said. 'Both those that Zeke has helped through his clubs and programmes, and those that he's yet to make an impact on. Anyone who has dealt with him in the past can be of some use to us.

See if you can get Alfie to watch their movements on CCTV. Find out what they were doing when Zeke was killed and where they were doing it.'

'What are you going to do with Clarissa?'

'I'll bring her in. See if she knows anything about the drugs. Leave that up to me.'

Jake sniffed. The air temperature in the room seemed to drop suddenly. 'And the sex trafficking in his business...?'

'Not possible. We have scarce resources as it is. I'd love to look into it, but we have to focus our time and effort on something that's more likely to be true.'

And it was all going so well.

Jake fought every ounce of instinct in his body not to roll his eyes. It was already becoming evident that Zeke Harrison had more secrets than he wanted people to know. He was a drug dealer, and now he was potentially adding human trafficker to his CV. And, out of the two, given Zeke's status amongst the gang members of Croydon, Jake didn't think it likely that any aggrieved dealers would seek retribution by placing a vice over his head.

That method of killing was far more advanced.

Far more...international.

'I think we should—' Jake began.

'It doesn't matter,' Payne snapped. 'You do what I tell you to do. Now go and do it.'

10

Wisdom

That evening, Jake unlocked the door, kicked off his shoes and hung his blazer on the coat peg fastened to the wall. The smell of cooked dinner lingered in the hallway and wafted through his nose, gently caressing his senses and stirring the beast in his stomach. On tonight's menu was chilli con carne. One of his favourites.

'Liz?' he called to a silent home. 'Liz, you all right?'

There was no response. Unlike her. She was usually there standing in the doorway at the end of the hallway with a smile on her face the moment he came in. But now—

The living room door opened, and his Elizabeth

appeared from behind it, pressing her finger against her lips. 'Be quiet! I've just got her down,' she said as she tiptoed her way towards him. 'If you wake her up, you're dealing with it.'

She wrapped her arms around his neck, kissed him, and then rested her head against his chest in a soft embrace. He buried his nose into her hair and sniffed, the smell of coconut filling him with a warmth that was accentuated by the heat radiating from her body. Mercifully, it didn't remind him of any of the perfumes he'd smelt in the Pink and Red Rooms.

'I wasn't expecting you so early,' she said as she pulled away from him. 'Otherwise I would have made dinner later.'

Jake shrugged. 'One of the beauties of working so close to the station, eh? How's Maisie doing?'

'Better. Your mum came over, gave me a hand. She said it might just be a cold, nothing to worry about. Right now Maisie needs to rest, so she's getting as much sleep as she can.'

Music to Jake's ears. For several reasons. Most important of which leapt from the forefront of his mind to his lips. 'Does that mean we get a decent night's sleep?'

A grin flashed on Elizabeth's face, her green-blue eyes shining beneath the hallway light. 'With any luck, you'll be able to get a full eight hours.'

Their first in as many months.

They moved into the kitchen, where they were greeted by the aromas of spices and meat. Jake adored Elizabeth's cooking, and he considered himself lucky that she was willing to do it every night for him while juggling the demands that came with having a newborn baby. Her sacrifices were not lost on him. They'd only been married seven months, but both were aware that making it a success was a two-way job. And, whenever possible, Jake was willing to step up and stand in.

Elizabeth moved towards the oven, switched it on, and then grabbed the baby monitor resting on the surface beside the gas hob. She turned the sound up and placed it back on the countertop.

She pointed to the fridge. 'Open it up.'

Jake didn't need to be told twice.

Inside was a bottle of Oyster Bay white wine, the most expensive and delicious wine they could afford without breaking the bank. Ever since Maisie had come along, their already-arid finances had completely dried up, and it was a rare luxury that they even had alcohol in the first place. Elizabeth opened an overhead cupboard and pulled down two glasses. She snatched the bottle from Jake and poured.

'I got it after the stress Maisie was giving me, think it's only wise.'

'Perhaps your smartest decision yet.'

God knew he needed a drink, something to relax him a little, something to burn the back of his throat and distract him from the events of the past day. And it would be even better with his wife by his side.

Elizabeth held out her hand. A cascade of bubbles rushed to the surface, gasping for air, jumping out over the side of the glass and landing on his fingers. 'For my strong superhero,' she said, giving him another kiss.

'You're going to have to stop calling me that. My ego's already big as it is.'

Elizabeth grinned playfully and moved over to the other side of the central island in the kitchen.

'How was work?' she asked.

Jake filled her in. As much as he could, at least. Keeping the details to a minimum, especially the gory ones. She didn't need to know that Zeke Harrison's brain looked like the contents of a Pot Noodle. That his eye sockets had burst leaving two dark, cavernous holes. That he'd vomited at the sight of it and now the images were etched into his memory, a permanent fixture in the gallery of his mind. She didn't need to know any of that. All she needed to know was that he was being pushed to the side by DCI Payne and his reluctance to show any trust in Jake.

'I'm sure there's a method to his madness,' Elizabeth said after he finished.

Why was everyone saying that? It was almost as bad as telling him there was nothing like learning on the job.

'But I think he's wrong.'

She rolled her eyes at him. 'You often think a lot of people are wrong. Doesn't make *you* right.'

Jake winked. 'Nine times out of ten it does. What do you think I should do?'

Elizabeth pondered for a moment, playing with her blonde hair and rolling it in her fingers until it tugged at her scalp. She took another sip of wine.

'You don't wanna upset them just yet,' she said. 'You've only just got there.'

'But...'

'But...you've always said you want to do what's right.' She hesitated, licked her lips. 'So do it.'

On the right side of Jake's cheek, just above the jawline, was a small scar he'd sustained after the family dog attacked him when he was a child. The scar prohibited any facial hair from growing around it. It was one of his biggest insecurities, and he always scratched it whenever he felt pensive, under pressure or nervous, hoping that he would by some miracle be able to scratch it off. Seventeen years later, he was still trying.

He lowered his hand, set it on the table, and looked into Elizabeth's eyes.

'You're always my source of wisdom.'

'I know.' She leaned over and kissed him on the lips. 'What would you do without me?'

That thought didn't even bear thinking about.

11

Can of Worms

The clock was ticking, and Anthony was still no closer to finding the hundred grand. His option pool was rapidly drying out. And, to make matters worse, word that something was wrong was beginning to spread furiously through the club like a sexually transmitted disease.

One of the girls from the Pink Room, Simona, had been seen speaking with the female police officer who'd visited earlier. What she'd said, he didn't know.

But he was going to find out.

Everyone in the Pink Room was under the strictest of instructions not to say a word to anyone. The punters. The police. Or even the other prostitutes working in the Red Room.

They were there simply to work, grind, and hand over all their earnings at the end of the day. Nothing more. Nothing less. He and Zeke had spent good money getting them over here, and carried a lot of risk with the decision. Trafficking humans across from Lithuania, Slovenia, Romania, Slovakia – "All the IAs", as he liked to call it – wasn't easy, nor was it cheap. But now the girls were in their debt, and they were slowly but surely paying it off. That is, until the goods became soiled and unusable – which usually happened as soon as the punters started complaining – then they were collected by The Milkman for a small fee and given a new lease of life somewhere. Possibly. Maybe.

He didn't know what The Milkman did with the girls after they were finished at Eloquence. Wasn't his job. Neither was it his place.

Anthony was in his office. The heavy, repetitive din from the music downstairs was reverberating around his feet, and making the keyboard and mouse on his desk shake. It was good to see Mason the DJ was able to follow orders; Anthony had given him instructions to play the music extra loud tonight.

To drown out the other noises that were about to come.

Anthony tilted forward on the chair and watched the rolling CCTV images play on the screen. His eyes fell on the top left quadrant. Two heavyset individuals wearing earpieces tucked into the backs of their shirts moved across the screen, their frames

74

so wide it looked like they were gliding. They stopped by one of the half-naked women in the shot. She was in the middle of serving drinks. Despite the CCTV's appalling pixel clarity, Anthony still noticed the fear in her eyes as she recognised who was standing in front of her and realised why they could possibly be there.

Anthony allowed himself a smile.

The bouncers ushered Simona out of shot and through the club, weaving their way towards his office. By his estimation, he didn't have long to prepare. Twenty seconds, thirty seconds, max.

He leapt out of his seat, grabbed the one opposite and moved it back a few feet so that it sat in the middle of the office. He kicked away a pair of trainers, a scrunched-up piece of paper and an empty Pepsi Max bottle to the outskirts of the room. Once the floor was clear, he rested his backside against the edge of the desk, folded his arms on his chest.

As soon as he was in position, the door opened.

Just in time.

Before him was Simona, in all her elegant beauty. She had a figure like a supermodel. Stick-thin, bony, curvy – not least because she and the rest of the girls were fed as little as possible – and her hair and make-up were flawless. It was good to see the time they spent outside of work hours was used effectively.

The girls were like products. And if the products were in immaculate condition, then more customers would want to buy them. And the more customers who wanted to buy them... Well, it was simple economics.

'Take a seat please, Simona,' Anthony said, gesturing at the chair. 'There's no need to look so worried.'

Her face told him a thousand concerns, and as she moved away from the slight security of the doorframe, stepping into the office, she wrapped her arms around her body and massaged the skin around her waist.

'Would you like a drink?' he asked, switching on his dinner guest voice, the one reserved for his monthly dinners with friends and politicians. Something to put others at ease before they discussed business.

Anthony propelled himself from the table and ambled towards the mini fridge at the back of his office. Inside was an assortment of drinks. Alcoholic, non-alcoholic, soft drinks, water. Even some apple juice. He removed a can of Coke and opened it in front of Simona, proving to her he hadn't poisoned it. The can hissed into life, and small bubbles fizzed around the rim. He passed it to her.

'Drink up. You must be thirsty. I've seen how hard you're working.'

Simona took a reluctant sip, more out of fear than any desire to quench a thirst.

'I suppose you're probably wondering why I brought you up here...' Anthony began as he rested against the desk. 'You're one of my top performing girls, and that deserves some recognition. Here at Eloquence we have a particular reward for the highest performer every month. It's called A Night with the Boss.'

Simona's English wasn't perfect. In fact, it was near non-existent, save a few words she'd picked up here and there, just enough to help her get by. And that was just the way he liked it.

'But first there's something I need to ask you.' He twisted on the table and grabbed his phone. Unlocking the device, he scrolled to the gallery and opened the latest video. He thrust it in Simona's face. 'Do you know who that is? Do you recognise her? She came in earlier, wanted to know about what had happened to Zeke. Her and her little boyfriend there are the police. They shouldn't have been talking to you. They shouldn't have been anywhere near the Pink Room.' He paused a moment to gauge Simona's reaction; the fear had multiplied, and she'd dropped the can into her lap, eyes glued to the screen. 'All I need to know is what you said to her.'

He pulled the phone away from her face, pocketed it and wandered behind her.

'I...nothing,' Simona said, her accent thick.

'You must have said something. You were talking for a long time. I've got all the footage on the phone if you'd like to see it again.'

'Please... No speak. I no say anything.'

'I don't believe you.'

Simona twisted in her seat, and the light caught on her shoulder. Her body was covered in a thin layer of sweat. Either he hadn't noticed it when she'd arrived, or it was a result of his intimidation, but the end result was the same: he felt himself getting hard.

'Please. Say nothing. No speak police. I tell nothing.' The inflections in her voice grew increasingly high-pitched, and her eyes looked like they were on the verge of tearing up.

Anthony moved round to her side. He crouched down and placed a hand on her thigh. The skin was smooth and soft, muscular from all the work she had to do on the poles. He slowly moved it towards her crotch. 'I won't be mad,' he told her, forcing himself to grin through the frustration. 'I won't be angry.'

But if you tell me No one more time I will beat the living shit out of you.

Simona licked her lips, spun the Coke can in her fingers.

'Please, I no—'

Anthony thrust his hand upwards and grabbed her throat. She let out a squeal and dropped the can in her lap, spilling bubbling liquid all down her thighs and legs, soiling herself.

'Dirty bitch! You make a mess in my office! Now tell me what you told the police!'

He squeezed. Harder. And harder. Simona gasped for breath and fought for purchase on her neck, but her wet fingers were too weak to make a difference.

'Tell me what you told them!'

When she didn't answer, he punched her in the face, his left hand colliding with her eye socket. Simona's head lolled to one side, and she cowered with fear. She tried to scream, but the sounds only made it as far as the walls. Nobody could hear her up here. Nobody.

'I'm going to give you one last chance!'

'Please, I no—'

That was it. He'd had enough. If a hand round her throat wasn't persuasive enough, then he'd have to try another method.

He yanked her from the chair and threw her against the table, her dazed and fatigued body colliding with the wooden edge. Once she was in position, he bent her over the desk and pulled down her underwear. Simona fought and punched and kicked with everything she had left to give, but her attempts at defending herself were useless. Anthony was too strong and he was able to subdue her with a jab in the kidneys.

After he'd beaten her into submission, he started with his trousers, one hand keeping Simona in place while the other fumbled with his belt buckle. Adrenaline, combined with an animalistic desire to overpower this woman, raced through him.

A few seconds later, his trousers were down and his rock-solid erection was standing to attention.

He was just about to insert himself into her when the door opened.

Standing there, caught in a snapshot of shock and confusion, was Arabella.

'What the fuck is going on?'

Anthony instantly covered himself, but by the time he pulled his trousers over his penis, she was gone. *Shit shit shit.* Leaving Simona behind to restore her dignity, Anthony hurried after Arabella, tearing out of the room and sprinting down the stairs to the club. He stopped in the door frame as soon as he realised he didn't stand a chance of finding her amidst the dark and dense crowds of middle-aged men perving and groping the women down there.

Beside him was one of the bouncers who'd brought up Simona. Anthony grabbed his sleeve.

'What're you playing at? Why'd you let her up?' His words were muffled and distorted over the beating sound of the base. When the bouncer didn't reply, he screamed, 'Find her!' in the man's ear.

At once, the bouncer started off, moving like a vending machine throughout the crowd, dispersing people left and right. As soon as he was out of sight, Anthony headed back upstairs, where he found Simona dressing herself.

'Get the fuck out of here,' Anthony yelled at her. He grabbed her by the hair and shoved her out of the room before she had time to react. He wasn't too worried about her; she was marginalised, cut off from the rest of the girls. It was unlikely she'd say anything.

And even if she did, nobody that could do anything about it would be able to understand her.

But Arabella...that was a can of worms he didn't want opened.

He started pacing from side to side, massaging his temples as he formulated a plan. By now his erection had gone, and he'd lost all desire to keep it up.

Then his phone rang. And if he thought there was the tiniest chance the erection may come back, it was destroyed the moment he laid eyes on the Caller

ID.

12

Snake in the Grass

DECEMBER 2008
SUNDAY

A bitter chill swept through the darkened streets of the Harengrove Estate. Great, looming shadows cast by the high-rise buildings shielded Jake from the weak sunlight above, worsening the effects of the cold he felt sinking into his skin. Giant plumes of smoke tumbled from his mouth as he waited outside. Pieces of litter, broken glass bottles, and clumps of some poor sod's brought-up dinner were scattered around the pavement around him. It was no secret amongst the community that the estate was rife with drug users and dealers, pariahs and criminals, all of whom were using the anonymity of the estate to hide their dealings. Austerity and changing social structures had meant that the people living in this part of town – the part frequented by more police than residents – were at the bottom of the pyramid. Poverty and injustice clung to every brick in the place, and it offered Jake a chance of perspective. He and Elizabeth were by no means rich – paying for a mortgage, a newborn baby and food for the both of them, on his salary, wasn't easy – but he could at least be grateful he wasn't living in conditions as bad as some of these individuals.

He reminded himself that, no matter how bad he thought he had it, there was always someone else worse off. And that was the saddest part.

The last few hours had been generous to him. After arriving early into the office, following a good night's sleep and a lengthy rest without too many disturbances, Jake had begun looking into the names of previous individuals Zeke had interacted with throughout his life. The list was almost endless – several mind-numbing pages at least. From everyone he'd attended school with, to the people he'd been arrested and imprisoned with, to all the young men and women whose lives he'd helped turn around.

A starting point had been difficult to discern.

But Jake had an idea. It would be pointless trying to speak with everyone, especially those down at the bottom of the list. Instead, he needed a handful of the top clients, those sitting on pole position in the starting line-up. And so he set about cross-referencing names of individuals who'd shown up – no matter how briefly – in every stage of Zeke's life.

Birth, school, drugs, prison, and more drugs.

Until he settled on one name: Leroy Jenkins.

Thirty-seven, five-nine, and clean-shaven – judging by the mugshot Jake had found on his file – Leroy had been known as a drug dealer and gangster throughout his life. He and Zeke had been at the same school together, been incarcerated together, and Leroy had even been a part of Zeke's several rehabilitation initiatives for young offenders and users. But there was a gap in the pair's history that intrigued Jake, startled the spidey-senses: according to the information he was able to find, Leroy had steered well clear of Zeke's multi-million-pound empire.

And Jake wanted to find out why.

He pressed the buzzer to Leroy's house again and stepped back, throwing his hands into his pockets, tucking his chin into his coat.

The door opened a few moments later, and he was greeted by a man dressed in a black vest revealing a set of muscular shoulders and arms covered in tattoos that were almost lost against the colour of his skin, and a pair of grey trousers stained with flecks of red paint. At the sight of it, Jake hoped it wasn't someone else's blood.

'Leroy?' Jake asked.

'Yeah. You that cop?'

Jake flashed his warrant card to prove his identity.

'You man better come in then. Freezing my bollocks off just standing here.'

Jake relaxed in the knowledge that Leroy was

able to feel the cold and that he wasn't a superhero. *Just a normal guy, like me.*

'You man want something a drink?' Leroy asked after he'd shut the door.

Jake told him he was all right for now, and then the two of them made their way towards the living room. A thick, dense wall of heat stifled the room and took Jake by surprise. It was a welcome change, but he knew that as soon as his body got used to it, the shock of stepping outside again would be enough to cause his heart to miss a few beats.

On the right-hand side of the room was a brown leather sofa, small chunks of it torn away from years of use, and a series of scratch marks ran down its side, evidence of abuse from a small dog or feline. In the middle was a glass coffee table covered in fingerprint stains – a SOCO's wet dream – and a television was fixed onto the wall on the opposite side of the room. Jeremy Kyle was in the middle of screaming at someone for having slept with their girlfriend's mum. Leroy grabbed the remote from the sofa, switched off the television and gestured for Jake to sit.

Jake did so carefully, perching himself on the end.

'So this about Zeke, yeah?' Leroy asked. The man dropped himself heavily onto the sofa and was immediately swallowed by the cushion.

'Have you heard the latest?' Jake asked, observing the series of dotted scars on Leroy's wrists.

'Word travels fast round here. Sure someone's

found out about you man coming round here too.'

'Is that going to be a problem?' Jake asked.

Leroy shook his head. 'I can defend myself. Plus I'm good with a lot of the guys round here. Made my peace with them.' Leroy snorted hard, bringing up a ball of phlegm, and rubbed the underside of his nose, then wiped it on his jogging bottoms. 'Whaddya need ta know?'

Jake pulled out his pen and paper.

'Your relationship with Zeke over the years, and whether you know of anyone who might have been involved with his murder.'

'I ain't a suspect then?'

Jake smirked. If he had a pound for every time he'd heard that question, perhaps in twenty years' time he'd be living the same lifestyle as Zeke himself. Jake asked him where he was on the night of Zeke's murder, and after Leroy explained to him that he was at a local Crystal Palace football game, followed by a heavy night's drinking session in the bar, Jake told him that he wasn't a suspect.

For now.

'Any help you can give us would be greatly appreciated,' Jake finished.

'Ain't much to know really.' Leroy sniffed again, harder this time, and adjusted himself into a more comfortable position. 'Me and Zeke knew each other from way back. Started dealing together. A bit of Mary, Charlie, Mandy. Shotting drugs to the fiends around the estate, till we both got nicked. We served our time, and then as soon as we got out, we both changed.'

'In what way?'

'You man ever been to prison?' Leroy asked and then kissed his teeth. 'Course you ain't. Look at you. Pretty little white boy like you. It's fucking chaos. Dirty place. Horrible. Ain't nothing else like it. We saw what went on in there, and we decided we ain't never going back. So we ain't dealing drugs no more, we ain't supplying nothing to no one.'

The look on Leroy's face suggested he'd seen things in the short time he was incarcerated that Jake would never see in a lifetime.

'I noticed that you're a part of Zeke's rehabilitation team at the local community centres and youth clubs...' Jake continued, moving the conversation along.

'The amount of kids on drugs is mad, man. Too many. And the amount of 'em that are dealing the stuff too...it's killing 'em. If the government ain't gonna give them the help they need, then some of us are gonna have to do it instead.'

It was a noble cause, definitely, but the rising tide of drug addiction and gang-related violence amongst young individuals in the area, and in the wider spectrum of London as a whole, was gradually becoming an epidemic, and Jake was beginning to feel they could only fight the tide with help from the powers above.

'When was the last time you spoke with Zeke?' he asked.

'Couple months ago now. Ain't seen from him or heard from him neither. As you man can probably tell, I ain't much arsed 'bout hearing him dying. If you man ask me, got what he deserved in a way. Some might say it was long overdue.'

Jake's ears perked up. Without his realising, he pressed the pen deeper into the pad, burying the nib in the paper. The intonation in Leroy's face made it seem like he was offering a friendly word of advice, a little too late, and to the wrong man.

'Can you tell me more?'

Leroy stroked the small dents in the crease of his arm, as if each one was a personal tragedy or piece of his history that was so far repressed in the back of his mind it needed rousing before he could begin.

'I ain't no snitch or nothing, but I changed after prison, man. Zeke didn't. I thought he had, but he was just the same. All his initiatives, all the BS he kept spouting off to the public, was horseshit. Ever since he got out of prison, Zeke's been funnelling drugs to the kids that have been coming to him for help. Same with his businesses. He just makes it look like he's cleaning up the streets. They're all a front for his drugs empire.'

That explains why a load was discovered at his house.

'As soon as I found out what else he was doing, I thought, nah fuck that, I'm outta here. Ain't want nothing to do with none of that.'

'None of what?' Jake asked, then realised he'd been so engrossed in hearing Leroy speak that he hadn't written anything down.

'Those girls that he's got working for him over at those clubs,' Leroy began, 'you man know where he gets them from?'

I have an idea but I'm waiting for you to tell me.

Jake nodded for Leroy to continue.

'They're all brought over on a boat, Eastern Europeans and that type. Cheap, slave labour, that kinda thing. Then they're forced to work in those places for him. He's trafficking them over so he can make a profit outta them.'

Jake felt a knot tighten in his stomach, and an image of the panicked girl Danika had spoken to yesterday appeared in his mind. Flustered, eyes widened, as if she were afraid the individuals in suits were going to take her somewhere. Abduct her. Beat her. Sexually assault her. Traffic her to another part of the country, continent, globe.

Danika's suspicions had been right.

'Who else knows about this?' Jake asked.

'Anthony Sharman, his business partner. I knew him from school, too. Only white guy in our class. Ain't difficult to forget a face like his. Plus he's a bit of a cunt, and you don't forget people like that.'

'Where are they getting the girls from? Who's supplying them?'

Leroy hesitated for a moment. His expression told Jake that he knew the answer, but something was holding him back. Fear, guilt. Or maybe Leroy was worried that, if he told Jake, then he'd suffer the same fate as Zeke.

'You can tell me,' Jake said, trying not to sound like a concerned father. 'If you give us a name we can find them, and we can also make sure the women get justice for what Zeke's done.'

'You know, there was a time when I would never have believed that. But now...you guys have been good to me since I got out...' Leroy inhaled sharply, held the breath in his lungs, and then let it out slowly. He rubbed his fingers together, like he was itching for a cigarette or something a little stronger to settle his nerves. 'I ain't ever met the bloke, but I know him by one name, innit. It's the name he goes by...'

Not in the mood to refuse any intelligence, Jake said, 'I'm sure it's something we can work with.'

Leroy licked his lips. 'They call him The Milkman.'

13

Chances of Survival

Arabella had never been as scared in her entire life as she had been in the last twenty-four hours. Walking in and catching Anthony attempting to rape Simona had disgusted her, sickened her, made her want to beat him to a pulp. But instead she'd fled and left Simona at his mercy – his terrible mercy.

She felt like her entire world was beginning to crumble. One boss was dead while the other one was a rapist and potential murderer. She'd defaulted on her last rent payment. Her bills were becoming astronomical. And there was even talk about the club shutting down – her income, her one revenue stream gone, just like that.

And what if the police started looking into her?

What if they started digging into her history? How much damage would those secrets cause to her reputation, her livelihood?

That didn't bear thinking about. Instead, since the morning, she'd busied herself with dredging up the dirt on Anthony and Zeke, finding out what the fuck they were up to.

She'd known all along that the Pink Room was different, that what was happening in there wasn't *right*. But she could never have comprehended the extent of the depravity of it all. She was naive, yes, should have known better. But now she did. Now the light of discovery was shining brightly on Eloquence and everything that was going on behind those brick walls.

It hadn't taken long to find out that, in the past year, Zeke and Anthony had been trafficking girls from all over Europe, exploiting them for money. Gradually at first, filtering them into the business, until recently – the past few months, at least – they'd brought in several more. All mid-twenties, all attractive, none of them speaking a hint of English – except perhaps *yes*, *no*, and the odd *thank you* here and there.

Now it made sense to her why they always relied on the bouncers to keep the punters in check. The girls couldn't protect themselves if they didn't understand what was being said to them – what was being *expected* of them. The thought made her body shiver and a cold flush sweep across her arms, forcing the hairs on her skin to stand on end in protest.

Arabella had accosted Simona after she'd finished her shift a few hours ago, and begged her to get into the car. Reluctantly, Simona had agreed, and after taking her to her house, where they were both on high alert for any signs of Anthony's presence, they'd discussed what had happened to her. Out of all the girls Arabella knew, Simona spoke the most English – which, by any standard, was still nothing at all. Eventually, after much deliberation and hesitation, Simona had given her an address: 59 Harringate Street. A small terraced property at the end of a long row of houses where all eighteen of the Pink Room girls were being kept, fed, and locked away. Out of sight and out of mind. The only contact with the outside world they were allowed was the journey from the house to the club, and back again. Meanwhile they were kept under close surveillance by Anthony's bouncers.

Arabella stepped out of the car and followed Simona to the house. The front door was decrepit, and the windows weren't much better. Chipped wood, overflowing vines, and a mass of detritus and litter discarded by passers-by covered the front garden like it was a landfill site. From the outside, the place looked abandoned, and she could only imagine what the inside was like.

The surrounding street was quiet, save for the sound emanating from behind the thick brick walls of the club round the corner. It was an ear-sore, and surprised Arabella that she could hear it from so far away, but then she realised the sound was second nature to the local residents.

Simona came to a stop beside the door, reached inside her bag and slid the key into the lock. She twisted slowly, tentatively, as if doing the opposite would cause the house to somehow explode.

When the door finally opened, Arabella was hit with the overwhelming smell of perfume. Thick, dense, almost like they were manufacturing it themselves. Eighteen girls, numerous shift patterns, eighteen lots of perfume and deodorants. It was almost toxic and clung to the back of her throat as she stepped in.

The hallway was dark, as was the rest of the house. The floor was dirty, and damp clung to the walls, while torn strips of wallpaper dangled loosely from the top. Fresh black bin bags were on the floor at the end of the hallway, waiting for someone to take them out at an inconspicuous time.

The sound of chatter and the noise of a television came from above, but other than that, silence crept along the walls. No talking, no laughing. No signs of human life.

Simona led the way, leaving Arabella to shut the door behind her. All ten of the girls who weren't on shift were inside the first bedroom. The dim light was on, and they were all hunched over the bed, the blue glow from the television dancing on their shock-stricken faces. Each of them looked afraid, terrified at their sudden entrance. Like they'd been expecting someone completely different – and not in a good way.

Arabella searched the room quickly, aware there were ten sets of eyes focused on her. She counted five sleeping bags, a handful of empty water bottles strewn across the carpet, and a dozen or so piles of clothes, the dirty and the clean almost indistinguishable from one another.

The sight of the dingy conditions made her sick with guilt.

'Don't worry,' she said aloud. 'I'm going to get you out of here. All of you. It's going to be OK, you're safe now.'

Arabella allowed Simona to convey a loose translation to the other Slovenian women in the room while she exited and made a call. Her eyes struggled to read Jake Tanner's mobile number from the card he'd given her, but after holding the card at several different angles to catch the light, she entered the number into her phone and dialled.

The call connected immediately.

'Hello?' his deep, strangely seductive voice answered.

'Detective Tanner, is that— Am I speaking with —?'

'This is Jake,' he replied. 'Who's this?'

'Arabella. From Eloquence. We spoke yesterday... About... *Zeke*.' She whispered her boss's name for fear that saying it loudly would raise his spirit from the dead.

There was a moment's pause. Then, 'Ah, yes. I remember now. How can I help you, is everything all right?'

Arabella stepped away from the bedroom door and made her way down a couple of steps on the stairs. Not that it mattered; no one in the room could

95

understand her that well anyway, but she felt safer knowing that she wasn't being overhead by anyone.

'I've got something I think you lot should know. It's about the Pink Room.'

'Right...'

'Well...they're all being trafficked. They're being holed up in a house, all eighteen of them. I found documentation in the offices earlier and I spoke with one of the girls. I think they need to be taken away from here.'

'What's the address?'

Quick and to the point. She liked that. She knew that trusting him was a good idea.

'Fifty-nine Harringate Street,' she answered. 'One more thing... I think Anthony Sharman is a very dangerous man. Last night, when I was at work, I saw him—'

Air escaped her lungs and she completely froze.

Standing at the bottom of the stairs, just stepping into the house through the front door, was Anthony Sharman. Alone. A sinister and insidious look swathing his eyes. Pitch-dark, as black as the depths of his soul.

'No!' Arabella screamed, climbing to her feet. 'No! No! No!'

She held her free hand out in front of her in defence, but it was no use. She tripped over the step and fell, the mobile spilling from her hand. Lying on her front, her body feeling trapped, as though there was an immovable force keeping her pinned in position, she screamed.

And then she felt his hands on her. Her ankle.

Her waist.

Was he coming to finish the job on her? Or was something worse going to happen?

She screamed again, this time at the top of her lungs. Before she had a chance to catch her breath, she was hoisted from the steps. She reached out and grabbed at the phone, but missed it. Her one lifeline, her one saviour.

Gone.

'Come here, you little skank!' Anthony yelled in her ear. His voice was different, evil, demonic. Unlike anything she'd ever heard before – and she'd had punters who'd lost control of themselves and shown their darker side. But it was nothing compared to this.

'No! No! Get off me!'

Where were the girls? Why hadn't they come to rescue her? Why were they still in the bedroom?

And then she understood.

The same reason Simona had returned to work for a full shift as though nothing had happened between her and Anthony in the office.

The same reason the girls had been sitting in the darkness, bunched up next to one another for protection.

Because they couldn't risk being caught on their own.

They couldn't risk stepping out of line.

Fear.

14

Cucumber

The television played, but she didn't pay it any attention. Just background noise, to take the edge off the profound silence that pervaded the house. Her mind was elsewhere. Wondering where her brother was. Wondering what had happened to Zeke. What sort of mess they were all caught up in. How it would impact *her*. Jobless, and being completely dependent on her brother's money meant that, if anything happened to him, she was up shit creek right along with him.

Over a day had gone by, and Clarissa still had received no word from Anthony. She'd called, messaged, begged. Nothing. And he still hadn't come home.

She hoped that nothing serious had happened to him. And she immediately dismissed any thought that suggested he'd found himself as dead as Zeke. He was fine, she told herself – *convinced* herself. Somewhat unsuccessfully. He was probably just busy at work, helping the police, making sure everything was in order. Capturing and arresting the people responsible.

Clarissa's stomach rumbled. She couldn't remember the last time she'd eaten. She didn't even know what time it was – except that it was dark outside, had been for hours, and that there was no sign of the sun coming up anytime soon.

Absentmindedly, her mind still consumed with crippling guilt and grief, she rolled herself off the sofa and shuffled through the darkness towards the kitchen at the back of the house. Keeping the lights off, she opened the fridge door, bathing the room in a soft blue light. She searched for the easiest thing to eat, the quickest thing to satiate the hunger. The last thing she wanted to devote any mental energy towards was tonight's dinner. There were more important things to worry about, more worst-case scenarios to create and let stew at the front of her mind, like all the rest she'd conjured up throughout the day.

She was suffering, and there was no one to talk to. Never anyone to talk with. No Zeke, and definitely no Anthony.

God, she wished she knew what the two of them had been doing, what in the hell they were mixed up with.

As soon as she found something to eat – a stick of cucumber that was just as lonely as her on the bottom shelf – a knock from the front door split the silence in two. She jumped, and her heart leapt into her mouth. Leaving the cucumber in the fridge, she headed to the door.

A part of her wondered whether it was the police again, coming to ask if she knew any more about the drugs they'd found in the house. But she'd already told them everything she knew about that, and they'd already let her go. So what could it—

She opened the door and, despite her mental space working at only fifty percent capacity, she was fast enough to immediately wish she hadn't. Three individuals, one in the front, two at the back, all dressed in balaclavas, were standing in front of her.

Before she was able to swing the door back in their faces, the man in front was on her. Hand over her face, disorientating her. Arm wrapped around her neck, suffocating her. Knee pressed in her back, buckling her legs. And then the other men were manhandling her, picking her up from the ground.

She tried to scream and thrash and fight her way out, but it was no use. She was weak, her body's strength dampened by her lethargy. As they carried her out of the house and into the back of a black van, she couldn't help but wonder whether eating the cucumber would have given her more energy, or whether it would have served a better purpose as a weapon to defend herself with.

Chances were now, she would never find out.

15

Top of the List

With the help of the blue lights flashing and the sirens blaring, Jake had been able to make it to 59 Harringate Street within a few minutes. It also helped that the roads were surprisingly empty for nine o'clock. Perhaps there was a new episode of *I'm A Celebrity...Get Me Out Of Here!* on, and the eight million people that tuned into it every night were glued to their television sets. Behind him was a series of three police vehicles, each carrying two uniformed officers. After receiving the call, he'd been cleared to attend the property without any senior oversight. According to DI Carmichael things were ramping up in the station, and they needed as much resources to focus on their existing efforts as possible.

It was bullshit and Jake knew it.

A missing person was an important and time-sensitive crime. The more people they had on the ground, the faster they'd find evidence and lines of enquiry. The quicker they found those, the quicker they'd potentially find Arabella. *Stupid bureaucracy*, he thought, and then policed himself. *Stupid fucking idiots*. That was better.

He pulled up outside the house, parking awkwardly, and sprinted towards the front door, the other officers close behind him.

The first thing Jake noticed about the house was the smell. And then the darkness of it all. The place looked as though it had been uninhabited for years, but the smell suggested the complete opposite.

'Police!'

A uniformed officer arrived behind him. In his hand he held a flashlight, and a cone of brilliant white light climbed the walls and illuminated the rest of the furnishings.

They checked the downstairs first, searching the living room, dining room and kitchen for signs of life. When they didn't find any, they headed upstairs.

Tentatively, aware of the creaking sound his feet made every time he trod on a step, Jake made his way to the top. On his right was a half-open door, a thin line of light defining it in the darkness. Jake came to a complete stop and kept the officer behind him in position too. They listened. Waited.

On the other side of the door was hushing,

shushing, the sounds of several individuals trying to remain discreet and hidden.

Jake placed a hand on the handle and pushed. His eyes fell on everything all at once. The cohort of girls sitting in the corner of the room, scrunched up together on the mattress, huddling in fear for their lives. The television playing in the background, images flashing rapidly on the screen and walls. The sleeping bags on the floor. The piles of clothes strewn all over the place.

Then he observed the girls. Each and every one of them looked petrified, though oddly calm. Almost as if they were expecting to be killed, and had come to terms with the fact a long time ago. The beam of light caught in the reflection of the bedroom window and almost blinded him, but he instantly recognised the girl Danika had spoken to. The one Arabella had called about. Simona.

'Police,' Jake said slowly, pointing to the word flashed across his police vest. 'Police.'

He turned his back on them, told the officer to wait by the door, and then made a call in the hallway.

'Danika?' he said as soon as she answered.

'Yeah?'

'I think you need to get down here.'

She arrived after just four minutes. Flustered, dressed in a police vest. She'd come with another uniformed officer, and in the short time it had taken her to arrive, the street was teeming with them. A cordon had been erected at both ends of the street, and blue flashing lights danced across the terraced houses like they were preparing for a disco. Officers were beginning to conduct their house-to-house enquiries up and down the length of the road. At last, some organisation, some semblance of logic behind DCI Payne's decisions.

'Where are they?' Danika asked as she approached the front door.

'They're upstairs in the bedroom still. They're scared. They don't know what's going on.'

'Sherlika to the rescue,' she said, flashing a wry smile as she slipped past him.

Jake followed her up the stairs. Within a few seconds of their arrival, the women in the room appeared to relax. Perhaps it was the presence of another woman – all the officers so far had been male, and they needed a face they could trust – or perhaps it was because Simona had spread the word that a female police officer was coming to speak to them.

Either way, Jake was pleased. They each looked more receptive to the idea of divulging information on what they'd seen. With any luck, at least one of them would know what happened to Arabella.

Danika approached the girls and started speaking to them in Slovenian. It was only the second time Jake had heard her talking in her native tongue, and it was a continual source of bewilderment. The language, the vocabulary, the sounds, the inflections in her voice. Languages were beautiful, and it was just a shame he couldn't speak anything other than

English. He'd like to have continued his German post-high school, but back then he hadn't found it cool, and had focused more time on playing with his friends. Something he regretted to this day.

After a few minutes of waiting outside the room, Danika emerged.

'Arabella was here,' she began. 'Simona said that last night Anthony tried to rape her in his office, but Arabella walked in before anything happened. Then she sprinted out of there, and nobody'd seen her until this afternoon when she bumped into Simona after her shift. Apparently Arabella had spent the day looking into the club's records, and found proof that the girls were being smuggled over illegally. Simona says she came back to help them. And then she called you.'

Jake nodded.

'But then Anthony turned up and he dragged her out of the house.'

'Was he alone?'

'They said he was. One of them came to have a look but ran back into the room after they saw him. These girls have never known anything other than fear. I'm worried for them.'

Jake empathised with her. He was worried for them too, but not nearly as much as she sounded like she was. For now, these girls were safe. But Arabella was still out there, somewhere. Right now she was his priority.

'Did any of the girls see where they went?'

Danika shook her head. 'They were all locked inside the bedroom.'

As expected. Jake took a step backwards and considered the places Anthony may have taken her.

The list was short, and the most obvious choice was at the top. Fortunately it wasn't that far away.

16

Clean Off

Anthony had never been to this part of town before. After receiving a text message from The Milkman arranging the meet, he'd entered the address into his state-of-the-art satnav and relied on the machine to get him there safely. The journey from the Whorehouse, as he liked to call it unofficially, took only twenty minutes. Arabella had screamed non-stop in the boot, begging for her life, pleading with him to let her go. She should have thought about that before she decided to interrupt him.

He'd soon blocked out the incessant whining and thumping, and focused on the task at hand: handing her over and settling the score. Once and for all.

Last night, The Milkman had offered him a deal.

One of his girls from the club, his best one, his money maker, the one who was going to earn the hundred grand debt back in no time. Arabella was the obvious option. She'd been the top girl for as long as Anthony could remember, and she had potential to go even further. Not to mention she could, and *would*, do anything if it meant a healthier pay packet at the end of the shift – he'd experienced first-hand what she was capable of.

Now it was time to clear his name, clear the debt over his head, and clear any ties linking him to The Milkman.

Outside, over a hundred metres away, was a row of disused factory buildings. Black patches stained the brickwork, weeds were growing along the bottom of the building, and the glass roofs were almost opaque with debris, limescale and soot. It was empty, desolate, and the nearest sign of life had been in the petrol station he passed three miles away.

Anthony was remotely aware that he was in the middle of the perfect place for a kidnapping.

Or the perfect place to be killed.

He dismissed the thought as he shimmied himself out of the car and hurried to the boot. The red light inside the car shone demonically on Arabella's face, accentuating her anger and fear. Her hands were bound with cable ties, while her mouth was taped using an adhesive he'd found in the office. It wasn't professional, but then again, neither was he; this was his first abduction.

And hopefully his last.

Avoiding all eye contact with her, unable to acknowledge the guilt he faced, he grabbed her hands and yanked her out of the boot. Her body, like a dead weight, slumped to the ground. No doubt she was making life as hard for him as possible.

He wrapped his arms around her, his breath fogging against the dark, starry night, and, hooking his hand beneath her armpit, he hefted her from the ground and dragged. As a woman who'd worked in clubs like Eloquence for a long time, she was no stranger to defending herself. So when she started thrashing and kicking out, her fingers loosely catching on his gold chain and watch, he wished he'd sedated her, knocked her unconscious – done *something* to suppress her survival instinct.

As Anthony arrived outside the factory, he slowed to a stop. Sounds echoed from inside. Voices, talking, coughing.

This was the place.

He backed into the doorway, pulling Arabella with him.

Then froze.

He didn't know what he was expecting to see, but he didn't think it would be The Milkman and four men dressed in black, surrounding his baby sister who was sitting in a chair attached to a table, her hand clamped inside a vice.

'Clarissa!' he yelled.

At the mention of her name, Clarissa's head rolled to one side, revealing her face. She was also bound and gagged. She'd been beaten, and a river of blood trickled down the side of her cheek and over her mouth. Her hand was buried too deep in the vice for him to be able to tell how much damage she'd sustained.

'Anthony!' The Milkman said, clapping his hands together. 'And who do we have here?'

It suddenly dawned on Anthony that he'd made a very big mistake. He looked between his sister and the girl in his arms. Both were the same age, both were the same height, build, both were his favourites – in different senses of the word – and both were blonde.

All of which met The Milkman's criteria.

He'd brought the wrong girl with him.

'Well, I do believe this is a good day.' The Milkman snapped his fingers and the four men hurried towards him. Two for Arabella, two for him. They were so strong that, even one of their arms was enough to overpower him.

'Bring him here,' The Milkman ordered.

The closer he got to his sister, the clearer her injuries became. The sleeve on her right arm was missing, torn all the way up to her shoulder, and there were small cuts and lacerations from where the sleeve had been roughly torn. But the worst of it was her hand. Dangling over the other side of the vice, blackened and bruised, the bones in her fingers all crooked and deformed. He could only imagine how many were broken and fractured, what immeasurable suffering she'd gone through. His sister, the one he was supposed to protect, the one he'd sworn he'd look after.

'You fucking bastard!' he spat.

'Where are your manners?' The Milkman asked as he stroked the vice. 'It's not my fault your business partner couldn't pay his debts. It's not my fault you couldn't pay in time. That lies with you. This is my consolation for the money.' The Milkman turned away from the vice and idled towards Arabella. When he reached her, the girl squirmed, but he paid her reaction little heed. He stroked her face and ran his fingers through her hair. 'I'm going to enjoy this one. Now I see why you brought her. Perhaps she really can cover the money.'

'Let Clarissa go,' Anthony called, unable to tear his eyes from his sister. She looked so weak, so broken.

'One thing at a time,' The Milkman said as he made his way back to the table. 'I wanted to bring you here so you could see this, so you could watch the debt get repaid.'

The Milkman placed a hand on the vice's handle delicately, as if he was caressing a loved one. Without warning, he twisted, hard, and Clarissa erupted into life and screamed in agony. Her cries split Anthony's head in two and punched him in the gut, almost doubling him over. Clarissa convulsed and her body turned rigid as she wrestled with the pain.

Anthony watched on helpless.

Until the unmistakeable sound of his sister's wrist bone snapping burst from behind the vice. Like the sound of a branch falling from a tree. The snap, the echo, and the absolute silence that succeeded it, save Clarissa's soft whimpers and heavy breathing.

'That's half the debt repaid,' The Milkman said, clapping his hands. He unwound the device, removed Clarissa's arm and shoved her on the floor.

At the sight of his fallen sister, something in Anthony changed. He tensed his muscles, kicked the shin of the man to his right, and then pushed him away. Breaking free from one, he punched the other in the face with a weak right hook and, taking his chance, sprinted towards his sister.

He made it all of ten feet before he was trampled to the ground, the weight of the big oaf crushing him from above grinding his face into the dirty, grit-laden concrete.

'Pick him up!'

Disorientated, Anthony felt a pair of hands swallow his arms and another grab his shirt. He was pulled from the floor and thrown in the chair, replacing his sister. Chest heaving, beads of sweat forming on his forehead against the cold, Anthony's eyes danced between Clarissa and Arabella.

Neither of them could help him now.

The two henchmen clamped his hands to either side of the chair using cable ties, and secured his ankles to the legs with industrial strength tape. With a clap of the hands from The Milkman, they disappeared and then returned a few moments later. As soon as Anthony laid eyes on it, his chest compressed and his stomach felt as though someone had kicked him in the groin repeatedly for ten minutes straight. It was unbearable. But it wouldn't be as unbearable as what was going to happen to him.

'You've seen my little creation before, haven't you?' The Milkman asked. 'I'd love to know what you think.'

Anthony didn't reply. His brain was too wild with fear to comprehend anything else. Both the henchmen were holding a head vice, identical to the one that had killed Zeke. Images of that night, lying face down in the dirt, hearing his friend's skull get crushed inside the device, flashed in his mind.

He felt sick. Like he was going to —

He vomited. An uncontrollable and involuntary reaction. The warm, putrid bile ran down his shirt, stung his throat, and the smell immediately made him gag.

He wanted to be sick again, but swallowed it down.

'Disgusting,' The Milkman said. 'Weak. Pathetic. Not even Zeke did that. What sort of man does that make you?'

The words didn't register. Instead, Anthony turned to face his unconscious sister. If he could look at one thing before he died, then he wanted it to be her. They hadn't necessarily seen eye to eye their entire lives – what siblings had? – but she'd been there for him when he needed it most, as he had for her.

Another clap of the hands.

Those hands. Those fucking hands. Anthony resolved that, *if* he survived, he was going chop The Milkman's bastard hands clean off. But slowly. Oh so very slowly.

That was the least he deserved.

113

The two henchmen started towards him, holding the vice in the air. Then they lowered it, his head slotting neatly into the circular cut-out.

Until the world went completely black.

17

Promises

At the club's entrance, Jake was welcomed by a six-five bouncer who'd probably spent more time in the gym than anywhere else in his life. Everything about him was thick. The head. The neck. The shoulders. The arms. The chest. The torso. Even all the way down to his calves and ankles.

With him was a handful of uniformed officers, each chomping at the bit to get inside and seal the place off. Police Sergeant O'Neill, a balding man in his early thirties, was the most senior officer, and was the one dishing out instructions.

'Who ya here for?' the bouncer asked as though half a dozen police officers turning up in the middle of the night was a common occurrence.

'We're here to shut this place down,' O'Neill said, and the bouncer stepped aside.

As soon as the man was out of the way, O'Neill tore through the entrance and, with the other officers following behind, disappeared into the building.

Jake was the only one to remain. He looked the bouncer up and down, gauging the man's height and weight. Quickly concluded that it would be a very one-sided fight.

'You seen Anthony tonight?' he asked.

'Nope.'

'Arabella?'

'Nope.'

'Any idea where they might be?'

'Nope.'

'Are you going to help me?'

'I'm not their personal assistants, I don't know where they are at every—'

A scantily clad woman, dressed in red lingerie and black high-heeled boots, burst through the front door and sprinted to the car park. Jake recognised her as the girl who'd approached him yesterday. Before he was able to react, another one appeared and sprinted off in the opposite direction.

'Shit,' he whispered vehemently.

Sprinting inside, sidestepping the overturned furniture and the police officer rolling on the floor with a suited gentleman, Jake saw what was happening. Their arrival had caused a mass exodus from the club. Everyone in the vicinity – men of all professions and women of one – were making a run for it, hurrying out of there as fast as they could.

One of the girls, whom Jake had seen yesterday holding a drinks tray, came running towards him. He stretched out his arms and tackled her to the ground, making sure his hands didn't land on any sensitive places in the process.

'Get off me!' the woman screamed. 'Please, I didn't do— I don't want to—'

Jake clambered off her and lifted her to her feet. He pulled her to the side of the room away from the chaos and raised his hands in surrender.

'We're not here to arrest you,' he said. 'We're trying to find Arabella. Have you seen her?'

Eyes wild, the woman shook her head. 'Is she OK?'

The low, heavy music playing in the background stopped suddenly, and was immediately replaced with the sound of the commotion and the police officers announcing their presence. Shame there was nothing that could replace the smell of sweaty middle-aged men.

'What about Anthony?' Jake continued, lowering his voice slightly. 'Have you seen him?'

'No. I ain't seen neither of them. Are they OK?' she asked. And when Jake didn't answer straight away, she threw her hand to her mouth and gasped. 'Oh my god they're in trouble, ain't they? Please tell me they ain't in trouble. What's happened to them?'

'We're trying to find out. When was the last time you saw either of them?'

The girl searched her memory for a moment. 'Yesterday,' she said eventually. 'After Arabella finished her shift. I can't remember when it was, but she came running down from Anthony's office and left without even getting her things.'

'What happened after that?'

The woman shrugged. 'Dunno, didn't see. Ant came down, looking all mad and pissed, and then he got a phone call so he went back upstairs. Got Dylan and Tyson to go and find her.'

'And did they?'

'Don't think so, nah. They came back in a huff a few minutes later. None of us girls was allowed to say anything though. And then they locked off the Pink Room, put Paddy in the Red Room to make sure none of us did nothing we wasn't supposed to.'

Jake nodded, smiled at her. 'Thank you. That's very helpful. Is there anything else you can remember at all? Was she due to work today?'

'Yeah. Think her shift was due to start couple of hours ago. Sunday evenings can be big nights for us. People coming in after a day with the family, pretending to be down the pub, watching the football with the lads. Instead they come here, and then they're all rosy the following morning for work. Arabella's our best and she always brings in the highest payers. Got a lot of disappointed clients when she didn't turn up today.'

'I can imagine,' Jake said, realising that he really couldn't. In fact, he couldn't imagine what mental and physical effect working in a place like this had on people. The behaviours they were subject to, the ideals that men had about them. It was perverse and made Jake's skin crawl.

By now, the commotion had diminished, and the

atmosphere returned to some sort of normality. The music was off, the floor was empty, and a few of the customers and girls – those who had nothing to hide or fear – had remained behind. Jake sighed as he looked out at them. There were a lot of questions to ask, a lot of answers to write down, and not a lot of time to do it in.

'You'll make sure nothing happens to her, won't you?' the girl asked.

At first her voice didn't register in Jake's head. It sounded like a distant echo, like the lecture Elizabeth had given him once after he'd decided to take Maisie to the park while she was asleep. Apparently it was wrong and dangerous, but they'd both needed the fresh air and exercise, so he'd switched himself off as soon as she'd started launching her tirade.

'Excuse me?' he said.

'You'll make sure nothing bad happens to her, won't you?'

Jake nodded and scratched the side of his face. He hated answering questions like that. Not just because they were impossible, but because telling people things they didn't want to hear never got any easier.

'We'll try our best,' he said.

That seemed to satisfy her, as she offered him a knowing smile and a dip of the head. Before she could disappear, Jake thanked her, gave her his card and instructed her to call if she remembered anything else.

As she wandered away, his phone rang. He answered without checking the Caller ID.

119

'Can you talk?' asked the voice. Deep, gruff, filled with attitude. Absolutely no chance of it being anyone else's other than DCI Payne's.

'I'm free, guv.'

'We need you to come back to the station if possible. We think we've found Arabella.'

18

Game Time

DC Alfie Cram had been examining various feeds of CCTV footage for the past hour, fastidiously combing through every possible detail that would, with any luck and hope, lead them directly to Anthony and Arabella. Reports had been coming in thick and fast about an erratic Mercedes overtaking, slamming on brakes, revving, beeping the horn, intimidating other road users. And, thanks to the countless cameras posted around the area, it hadn't taken long for Alfie to find a starting point.

'The footage went cold around here...'

In the middle of the briefing room's largest wall, projected onto a canvas screen, was a map of Croydon. In his hand, Alfie held a pointer, and the red dot shook nervously as it highlighted a small residential street on the east side of the town.

'Cell Site is picking up Anthony's mobile number here.' Alfie pointed to an industrial area over a half mile from the residential street. 'From what I can tell, the number has been there for the past twenty minutes. We're in the middle of trying to find out what's there, and who owns the properties. From this satellite image, it doesn't look like anyone's inhabited it for a while.'

'Perfect place for a drug factory, then,' DS Coker said.

Jake rolled his eyes and focused on DCI Payne, who'd stepped in front of the projection and dismissed Alfie back to his seat, like he was a school child who'd just finished reading from a presentation about igneous rocks.

'I've been discussing with the strategic firearms commander,' Payne began, 'and he's going to give me a call when we're ready to go. As soon as he does, I want you all to head to this address, following behind the armed officers. When we get there, they're going to scope out the place. Because it's such a large area, the territorial support group will be with us as well, covering off potential exits here, here and here.' Payne pointed to three arterial roads leading into the estate. 'I want you all dressed in your police vests. We know from intelligence and evidence seized in Zeke Harrison's home that Anthony may very well be armed, so we need to be prepared.'

The evidence Payne was referring to was a Glock

17 found beneath Harrison's bed, something Clarissa repeatedly denied having any knowledge about.

'We don't know what Anthony Sharman's state of mind is like, but we have to anticipate that he may be very volatile. And we can't rule out the possibility that he may be with others. The reasons for Arabella's abduction are unclear.'

'Actually, sir,' Jake said, raising his voice so everyone could hear him, 'that's not quite true.'

'Oh?'

Jake turned to Danika, and allowed her the floor.

She cleared her throat before beginning. 'Last night, Anthony Sharman attempted to rape one of the Slovenian girls, Simona. She's the girl I spoke with earlier in the day, as part of our questioning process. She said that Anthony beat her and tried to get her to—'

'What's this got to do with Arabella?' Payne asked, checking his watch.

'She walked in on it happening,' Jake interrupted, sensing that Danika was getting flustered at their boss's asinine behaviour. 'It was in our report. Everyone should know this?'

Jake said it more as a question, but the reaction of everyone in the team told him they were taking offence, that he was throwing them under the bus – including the guv.

'So what you're saying is,' Payne began, 'now Anthony's got to silence her for what she's seen, possibly the same way he did with Zeke.'

'Or it's got something to do with The Milkman...'

'Who?'

Jake looked around the room. He was met with blank expressions.

Does no one read a fucking word of anything I write?

'Zeke had links with him. Accused of trafficking the Eastern European girls into the club and throughout the rest of Zeke's businesses. Zeke was involved in a lot more than just drugs, guv. He was deep in debt, from the looks of things. I think now maybe it's been passed on to Anthony.'

Jake's revelation seemed to shock everyone in the room, as if he'd finally convinced them he could be a detective – and a good one, at that. But before anyone was able to react, Payne's phone rang. As he answered he held his finger in the air, silencing the room.

When he finished, he simply left, tacitly expecting everyone else to follow him out.

And they did. Because they knew it could only mean one thing.

Game time.

19

Alone

In all her years as an escort, stripper and pole dancer, Arabella had never seen anything as depraved as this. And that was saying something. Anthony's head was trapped inside a metal box, and his sister was semi-conscious on the floor, the rise and fall of her chest offering the only evidence to suggest she was still alive.

What was going to happen next to them, she didn't know. And she didn't want to stay around long enough to find out either.

Worse, she didn't want to know what was going to happen to *her*.

The man wearing the brown leather jacket came towards her, a wide smile stretching the sides of his face like a Halloween puppet. She could feel his eyes surveying her, obsessing over her, undressing her as he approached.

This was it, she thought. She was going to die, get raped, beaten, stabbed, have her head crushed in a—

'What's your name?' he asked, taking her by surprise.

She was so bewildered that the question didn't register, and it wasn't until he asked again that she answered with her name.

'Not your stage name, your *real* name.'

Real name? It was so long since she'd last used it, it was almost like an old friend, lodged somewhere in the recesses of her mind.

'Natalie,' she said slowly. The word felt disgusting to say.

'Very good, Natalie. Let me ask you: do you care about Anthony over there?'

Of course she did. On some level. He'd given her the job in the first place, pushed all the rich punters her way, made sure she had extra tips, defended her if anyone kicked off. But he was also a monster, a demon. He'd shown his true colours this evening and the last, and they were as black as his heart. He was ready to trade her off for his sister.

'Do you care about him?'

She was flummoxed by the question.

Brown Leather rolled his eyes and turned his back on her. 'Only one way to find out,' he said as he started towards Anthony.

When he arrived, he placed his hands on the top of the box, wrapped his fingers around the vice's

126

handle on the front, and started rotating.

Anthony, who'd been almost comatose, sprang into action, and started writhing and wriggling and kicking his legs out, forgetting that he was prohibited by the cable ties around his ankles. Muffled screams permeated through the metal. Arabella didn't know what was going on inside the box, but if it was anything like the contraption they'd used on Clarissa's hand…

A lump caught in her throat.

She couldn't stand here and watch him die. It would weigh on her conscience too much, eat away at her every waking thought.

Using the acronym SING – a handy technique she'd learnt from her favourite film *Miss Congeniality* – Arabella broke free from the henchman's grip.

Solar plexus.

Instep.

Nose.

Groin.

The only problem was, there were two of them, and her blows on one were impeded by the other, who was far quicker to react. The second man grabbed her arm and yanked her backwards as she tried to flee, her legs barely having enough time to get working.

She collapsed to the floor. Damp and chill hugged her back, and a dull ache throbbed in her skull. She hit the deck so hard it almost knocked her unconscious, and sent the air from her lungs barrelling out of her chest.

With the inside of the factory spinning, she was

dragged along the gravelled concrete towards the muffled screaming and shouting. The man dragging her let go beside Anthony's feet. Inadvertently, amidst his thrashing, his toe kicked her in the face. The blow landed cleanly with her bottom left jaw, knocking the filling she'd recently had fitted onto the concrete.

'You little sket!' Brown Leather yelled, bending down to her face and pulling her hair back until it started to tear from her scalp. 'Who the fuck do you think you are? You're gonna pay for—'

He stopped abruptly and looked away, into the empty space behind her. His eyes moved left and right and the muscles behind his ears twitched like an alert dog's. If it hadn't been for the clean-shaven jawline and big nose, she would have guessed he'd been a Labrador in a previous life. Or perhaps a Rottweiler. Except right now a pug was more apt.

The atmosphere in the factory stilled. The screaming, the grunting, the yelling abated. Even Arabella noticed she was holding her breath, straining her ears for the source of distraction.

And then she noticed it. The sound of sirens, growing increasingly louder with each passing second.

The police.

They were coming to save her.

'Shit!' Brown Leather cried. He rushed away from her and grabbed his things from the table. He gave another command and, the next second, the two thugs were on her, one of them loading her onto his shoulders.

Arabella bounced up and down against the man's back as they sprinted out of the factory, leaving Anthony and Clarissa behind. Whether they were dead, she didn't know.

But now she was alone. With five men. Who were clearly capable of extreme levels of violence.

And she wondered, as she was thrown into the back of their van, stationed on the other side of the building, how long it would be before she became their next victim.

20

Team Player

DECEMBER 2008
MONDAY
As Jake floored it towards the industrial estate, he was acutely aware of the invisible ticking clock chasing them. There was a small team of four police vans carrying several units of armed officers, three liveried emergency response vehicles, and an ambulance trailing behind. The factory was only a few miles away outside Croydon, but it was the longest fifteen minutes of Jake's life. Images of Arabella, tied up somewhere, beaten, bruised and left for dead, appeared in his mind.

But he couldn't think like that. Pessimism would get him nowhere.

Sitting beside him was Danika, tapping her fingers on her knee, bouncing her foot up and down on the floor mat. They sat without speaking, though conversation would have been impossible anyway because of the sound of the engines and the sirens around them.

It was just after midnight when they arrived. The temperature was a few degrees below, and a thin veil of frost had settled on the untouched landscape of concrete and overgrown weeds that surrounded the factory. Overhead, the moon tore through thin strips of clouds, bathing the area in a ghostly white glow, but further in the distance was a wall of dark grey. Forecast: snow. Lots of it. A beast from the east, it was being called. The first time snow had fallen this far south at this point in the year since the turn of the century.

Jake and Danika were last to pull up, and as soon as they came to a stop, the armed officers, clad in their protective clothing, hauling their SIG MCX 556 Carbines in their arms, rapidly disembarked the vans and sprinted towards the factory.

The building itself was a massive structure, over a hundred feet tall and triple that in its length. Derelict, it didn't look as though it had been used in years. Either side of it were the graves of where other buildings had once been, and large piles of rubble and debris earmarked the headstones of these fallen structures.

The small army of authorised firearms officers dispersed and circled the perimeter of the factory, ten to the right, ten to the left. By the time Jake was out of the car, they were already in position, feeding back everything they saw.

Jake and Danika, along with the other detectives with them, were dressed in stab vests, and tuned into the radios so they could hear everything that was being said.

'There's a white Mercedes Benz over here,' one of the AFOs said over the static. 'Registration ends in 5DV. Boot open, empty. Rest of the vehicle is empty. Proceeding to the factory now.'

Jake recognised the number plate as Anthony's. A screenshot printed from one of the speed cameras that caught it had been stuck to the wall in the incident room for the past hour, serving as a constant and pertinent reminder of their objectives.

'Approaching now,' the officer whispered through the mike.

There was a brief moment of absolute silence as Jake and everyone else in the vicinity waited.

And waited.

Until screams of 'Armed police!' ripped through the still air and echoed around the structure. The noise spilled out of the holes in the building and leaked all the way to Jake.

'Put your hands in the air! Hands in the air where I can see them!'

Adrenaline surged through him while he waited. Rubbing his thumb and forefinger together, he kept his eyes trained on the building, waiting for confirmation to enter, to find and rescue Arabella, to put an end to this.

The confirmation came a few moments later.

Jake raced towards the factory, only slightly weighed down by the vest, and entered behind a uniformed officer. He bumped into a logjam of detectives who, upon seeing the crime scene, had stopped in their tracks. Jake shuffled to the side to gather a better view.

In the middle of the space, surrounded by the armed officers, was Anthony, alone, dressed in his designer suit, strapped to a chair beside an empty desk, a giant box placed over his head.

'Not again…' Jake whispered to himself.

He hoped they weren't too late. But if they were, then he was prepared – mentally and physically – for the sight of the body. The blood, the mess, the brain matter.

Already the sensation was returning, growing in his stomach with every second he spent looking at the body.

Jake felt a nudge in the back. A group of paramedics had arrived and barged past him. Within seconds they were on Anthony, checking for a pulse, gradually beginning to unwind the device and remove the box from his head. The contraption was evil, an example of the deepest depths of human depravity. It was abhorrent, and —

A knot formed in Jake's stomach and a great weight pressed on his head, crushing from either side of his skull. The world seemed to turn dark. A sharp, jagged pain ripped through his chest, and without warning, his body turned cold, his surroundings slowly melting into one another. It was happening again, gentle this time, in comparison to how much worse it could have been. An anxiety attack, induced by a sudden surge of stress and shock. They'd started after he'd barely survived an avalanche a few years ago while on a university ski trip with his friends. Buried beneath a three-foot-deep layer of snow, he'd felt overwhelmed, trapped, aware and terrified of imminent death. But by some miracle, he'd managed to crawl to the surface and drink in great swathes of oxygen, of life. The attacks had originally been frequent after the incident, but as time wore on – and with a little professional help – they were showing signs of abating, and he was growing more confident in combating them.

But this was the first time one had sprung up on him so violently.

Regulating his breathing, Jake took a step back from the crowd and turned away from the crime scene. He bent forwards and rested his hands on his knees.

In, hold, out.

In, hold, out.

In.

Hold.

Out.

Finally, the weight against his chest eased, the pressure on either side of his skull tapered off, and his body returned to a normal temperature. The attack had gone almost as quickly as it had started.

In the short time he'd been indisposed, the armed officers had made their way around the factory and cleared it, and the paramedics had delicately removed the box from Anthony's head, placing it on the floor a few feet away from his body. Jake was relieved to see that, on the surface, Anthony was alive and well, save for the trickles of blood running from his ears. However, as to the extent of the injuries he'd sustained internally – the potential brain damage, the lifetime of stress and ATSD of having to live with his injuries and the experiences of how he got them – they wouldn't know until he was in a hospital bed.

But they couldn't wait that long.

They needed information.

Jake hurried over. Anthony's head was slumped forward, resting peacefully against his chest. His breathing was slow, extremely slow, and appeared laboured, like each breath was causing him immeasurable amounts of pain. Jake tapped one of the paramedics on the arm.

'Can he talk?'

The paramedic looked at him bleakly. 'Not a chance, mate. We've gotta get him to a hospital immediately. Right now it's the best chance you'll have of speaking to him at all.'

Shit. Their one witness, the one person who'd seen everything, heard everything, knew everything, was about to be whisked away to a hospital, where God only knew how long it would be until they could interview him.

The Milkman was gone. So was Arabella. And if they were together, then Jake knew the chances of them finding her were slim.

They had no idea where to look.

135

No idea even where to begin.

Buried deep within the bowels of Eloquence, Police Sergeant O'Neill, along with two of his most trusted colleagues, were busy rummaging through the confines of Anthony Sharman's office with a fine tooth comb, their bodies bumping into each other with every movement. By now, the entire club had been evacuated, the patrons and employees spoken to, and a perimeter set up around the property.

Eloquence was his domain now.

'Anything relating to criminal behaviour, I want it seized,' O'Neill told his constables, Maguire and Jones. 'Bank statements, print outs, emails, communications, receipts, little love letters he wrote to someone else, little love letters he received from someone else. I want it all seized and bagged up. The more work we do here, the less work the men in black will have to do when they finally arrive.'

His best and brightest gave him a gentle grunt each, their enthusiasm understandably low. It was the middle of the night, and the last thing they wanted to be doing was search through mountains of paperwork. Especially in a place like this. From what he knew about his boys, they would have preferred to be downstairs, listening to the music, blowing off steam instead of being in this windowless sweat box.

'Chop chop!' he shouted, clapping his hands.

For a business that was possibly a front for organised crime and money laundering – as was the rumour coming from above – the office was surprisingly squalid, and looked as though it hadn't been renovated since its original construction. How someone could sit in there for nine hours a day, he didn't know. The floor was sticky. The decor looked, and made him feel, depressed. And the low light made his eyes ache. But the smell was the worst. Damp, sweat, stale tobacco, rotting food in the fridge. It was repulsive, and clung to the back of his throat.

Tucked into the corners of the room, either side of the small kitchen area, were two filing cabinets, while another smaller one was shoved beneath Anthony Sharman's wooden desk. All unlocked and ready to be pilfered. With his constables searching through the cabinets by the sink, O'Neill pulled the chair out from beneath the desk and sat. As he bent over, ignoring the pain flaring up in his lower back, he yanked the bottom shelf open, revealing a small combination safe.

'Jackpot, lads,' he said.

No expert in cracking safes, he placed it on top of the desk, ready to be inspected by the people who were paid to do so. Then he turned his attention back to the filing cabinet. But his search was over as soon as it had started. He found nothing except for a pen lid and a Kit Kat wrapper.

'You got anything?' he asked his officers.

Nothing.

Disappointed, O'Neill leant back in the chair, fingers knitted together. He cast his gaze about the room, imagining, wondering where he'd hide his illicit activities if he were a criminal mastermind. But it was by sheer chance that he found it.

As he shifted himself into a more comfortable position on the chair, his foot knocked the back end of the filing cabinet. The sound it produced was hollow, empty.

Intrigued, O'Neill bent down, crawled on the thick, filthy carpet, and pulled the cabinet away from the wall. There, he found it.

The back of the cabinet had been cut out and replaced. A hole had been drilled into the cutting to create a small handle, large enough for a pinkie finger. O'Neill plugged his inside and pulled the metal away.

Staring up at him was a mobile phone, a Sony Ericsson Xperia 1 – one of those new ones on the market he'd heard so much about – and a small notebook, bulging at the seams. Pulling his forensic gloves lower down his wrist, O'Neill removed the contents and started searching through the notebook. It was littered with print outs, documents, receipts, emails, bank statements. Everything they needed, all in one place.

'Think this is the real jackpot, lads,' he said enthusiastically. His seniors would love this. Think of the praise, the commendations.

'What's it say?' asked Maguire.

O'Neill ignored him and read the first document. An email chain between Zeke Harrison and an Undisclosed Recipient.

'£45,000,' he began. 'Two girls. One brunette, one ginger. Discreet transit, delivery in two weeks.'

A moment of silence fell on him as he processed the information.

'What do you think it means?' asked Jones. The youngster had only been in the force less than a year, and was an incredibly street smart person, an accolade that'd helped him shine, but sometimes his idiocy baffled O'Neill.

He looked up at Jones. 'You know, if you had a brain you'd be fucking dangerous, kid.' He clambered out of the hole beneath the desk and brushed himself down, said, 'Carry on with what you're doing. I need to make a phone call.'

Alfie had always found that time seemed to fly past whenever he was at his happiest – meticulously viewing and reviewing hours of CCTV footage. It was like stalking people, observing them through a lens, and he often spent the time trying to figure out what their lives were like. The hundreds of people stepping on a train, oblivious that there was a knifed attacker amongst them. The businessman, the school teacher, the yoga instructor, the musician and band manager, the struggling student. The human boiling pot of professions.

Sometimes when he worked he liked to think of himself as a lone wolf, a solitary huntsman who didn't need a team behind him. Not just because he liked to be left alone, undisturbed, so he could get on with what he needed to, but mostly because he didn't trust anyone else to do the job as thoroughly and comprehensively as him. As a result, he lived and breathed by the mantra that, if he wanted a job done properly, he should just do it himself. He didn't care about praise, notoriety or any of the other bullshit fluff that came from doing the bare minimum required – his job. He just did it for the thrill of it, and because he knew, selfishly, that he could do it better than anyone else.

There was no 'I' in team, but there certainly was in Alfie.

But in the past two hours, however, he'd achieved very little – at least, by his standards, it was an inconsiderable amount.

'What're you talking about?' Carmichael began, placing a firm hand on Alfie's shoulder. 'Not only have you managed to find the vehicle they escaped in, but you've simultaneously managed to find out where the slimy bastard is heading.'

Alfie shrugged. Tomato, tomato.

'I can do more.'

'That I'm sure you can, but right now I just need you to keep an eye on their movements. If they deviate their path, let me know.'

'What about the phone and intelligence that uniform found at the club? Need me to do anything with that?'

Carmichael shook his head, squeezed his shoulder. 'No need, boyo. Digital forensics team are on it. From what I hear they're a lot like you.'

'In what way?'

'Awake twenty-four hours of the day, don't get out much, probably still virgins. And even if they do sleep they're still glued to the computer screen.'

If Alfie's mind wasn't as focused on monitoring The Milkman's movements as it was, then he would have come up with a witty response, or perhaps a simple 'fuck you'. But sadly he could do neither, because, as soon as Carmichael finished speaking, Helen Spencer arrived, wearing a motherly smile on her face. In one hand she carried a can of Diet Coke, and in the other she held a sheet of paper.

She slammed the document on the desk.

'What's this?' Carmichael asked, clearly too lazy to look at the sheet and find out for himself.

'DFU hacked into the phone that was found in the filing cabinet of Sharman's office. It was registered to Zeke Harrison. He possibly left it there for safe keeping. On the phone were hundreds of texts and emails and photos, mostly from The Milkman. Thanks to their wizardry and black magic, DFU were able to locate where the texts were coming and going from.' Helen reached across both of them and prodded her chubby finger at the sheet. Her fingernail was pointing towards a satellite image of an industrial estate. 'They reckon this is a potential warehouse The Milkman uses for trafficking the women into the country.'

'Where is it?' Alfie asked, his eyes scanning over the road names and numbers.

'Dover,' Helen replied.

Exactly where he believed the black Transit van was heading.

'I'll inform Kent Police,' Carmichael said.

'Don't forget Jake and Danika,' Alfie added, keeping his gaze fixed on the map. 'They'll need to know as well.'

Look at you, he thought. *Thinking of others. Maybe you can be a team player after all.*

21

Sleep

They'd been driving for the past twenty minutes. At least, that was what her internal clock told her. For the first ten, she'd started counting the seconds in her head, and every time she reached sixty, she extended a finger on her hand. Then things got tricky. With the constant swinging left and right, and the loud, disorientating conversations coming from ahead, she was unable to keep track.

She had no idea where they were, and she had no idea where they were going.

Arabella was in the back of the Transit van, her hands and feet bound in front of her with cable ties. Beside her, head lolling from side to side like an empty bottle blowing in the wind, was Clarissa,

Anthony's sister. They'd only met on one other occasion – at a house party hosted by Zeke – and they'd immediately seen each other as a threat. One was going out with the host, while the other one wanted to. But right now, if Arabella could wake her, then they were each other's only chance of survival.

Sitting alongside them, pressed against the wall nearest to the drivers, was one of Brown Leather's men. His attention distracted, his head peering into the cockpit.

In the back of the vehicle it was almost pitch dark, and nearly impossible to discern any noticeable features – anything she could use to identify the man if she ever needed to.

Not only was she devoid of an awareness of time, but she was also devoid of light. And right now, everything relied on her touch and other senses.

'How long?' the man asked.

'An hour,' came the reply from the front.

An hour. Where was an hour away from London? Her mind drew an immediate blank.

'What are we going to do?'

'I don't know. I'm still working on it.'

'We could –'

They hit a pothole and the entire van shook. Angry shouts and protestations erupted from the front of the van. Clarissa's body fell onto her, leaning against her like a paralytic drunk.

And then the car skidded to a halt.

They'd stopped.

Why?

'The fuck're you doing?' the man in the back screamed. 'Keep driving!'

Confusion fell on the car. Arabella held her breath, listened. Somewhere in the background, she thought she heard the sound of a motorway. Distant, but close. Like it was only a few hundred yards away. The sound of hundreds of tyres rolling across the tarmac.

The sound of civilisation, of escape.

Arabella nudged her shoulder into Clarissa, attempting to rouse her. When that didn't work, she used her head, gently bumping it into Clarissa's.

'Hey,' she whispered in the girl's ear. 'Hey! Wake up!'

But before she could, the man in the back stormed past, accidentally stepping on Arabella's foot, and hopped out of the van. The driver and passengers followed suit.

As the door opened, a flurry of snow fell on top of her, thrown in by a sudden gust of wind. Her eyes adjusted to the light coming from outside, and through the gap in the half-opened door, she took in her surroundings. They were in the middle of an anonymous stretch of road, and all five men were surrounding something on the ground.

'The fuck is that?' one of them asked.

'It's a deer.' Brown Leather bent down and placed a hand on the animal. 'Stupid bastard,' he said. 'Thing just ran out in front of me. Fucking thing's still alive.'

She stopped listening to them. Realised that if

145

she was going to stand any chance of surviving, she needed to act.

And she needed to act now.

In one final attempt, she shoved Clarissa awake. Unsuccessfully.

It was settled, then.

She was going to have to do it alone.

Feeling a new sense of determination consume her, she struggled to her feet, and charged out the back of the van. As she soared through the air, her momentum carried her into the back of man who'd tied her up. He stumbled forwards and tripped over the deer.

But she paid him no heed. Turned her back on them and hopped towards the front of the van. Impeded by the ties around her ankles, she staggered to the door, yanked it open and clambered inside. Ignoring the safety of the seatbelt, she reached for the keys, twisted them in the ignition, and—

An arm wrapped around her throat and hefted her out of the car. She clawed for a purchase on something, anything that would offer her even the slightest chance of defending herself, but all she found was air.

'Get off! Get your hands off me!' she screamed.

As she was dropped to the ground and dragged along the concrete by her hair, she screamed in agony, her shrieks piercing the air. All those times she'd been attacked, molested, groped insidiously by her customers, she'd had the bouncers to rescue her. But where were they now? Where were the skills she needed to protect herself? They hadn't worked against Anthony and they weren't working now.

'Pick her up!' Brown Leather yelled. His voice was hoarse, impatient.

One of the men hooked their arm beneath her and lifted her from the ground, away from the tarmac and onto a field of grass. It was then that she noticed the cold, the bitter chill biting into her fingers and exposed flesh. A wintry grave.

'Please!' she screamed. 'Please don't do this!'

'On your knees,' Brown Leather instructed.

Arabella did as she was told.

'Please...' she begged, her voice weaker now. 'Please don't do this.' She breathed heavily. Her eyes stung as tears formed and started down her cheeks. 'Please... Please...'

She'd failed. And now she was going to die. She could only hope that it was over quickly for her. That it was over quickly for Clarissa too.

A brief pause, punctuated by the sound of a gun cocking.

She looked around her. At the walls of black surrounding them, the stencils of trees and bushes silhouetted against the darkness. And then, for the first time, she heard the sound of the motorway properly, of cars streaming past, of people getting from A to B. Further away than she'd first assumed, but a noise she'd taken for granted nonetheless. And then, on the flip side, the absolute stillness of it all. The silence, the peace, the tranquillity. A sensation she'd never experienced before on this scale.

She felt the gun press against her head. It's cold

metal burning the back of her scalp. Tears formed in her eyes. This was it. Her final moment.

She started counting in her head naïvely, as though it made a blind bit of difference, as though they would somehow adhere to her own countdown of death.

Three.

Go on, do it.

Two.

Get it over with.

One.

End everything.

The hammer clicked into place, but the gun misfired.

A lifeline.

But before she could capitalise on it, she was hit round the back of the head. A searing pain and brilliant explosion of white light flashed across her vision. She screamed and collapsed to the ground, her face melting into the snow-covered grass.

'What the fuck are you doing?' Brown Leather asked.

Somehow, still conscious, yet through half-opened eyes, she watched the leader of the group race towards her killer. Brown Leather snatched the gun, inspected it, and hurried over to the deer. The animal was still lying in the road, it's body spasming as it clung to its last iota of life.

Brown Leather hovered over the animal, pointed the gun at it, and fired.

The spasms stopped.

The sound reverberated around the field, but

was quickly drowned out by the traffic.

'Do I have to do everything myself?' he asked. 'Had to put the little bastard out of its misery.'

Arabella froze as she realised he was coming towards her. That she was next. That he was going to shoot her, just like he had that deer. Both of them injured, defenceless, unable to move. She could feel her blood rapidly spreading across her head, trickling down her neck, seeping through her clothes, fighting against the cold.

Her body was warm now. Pleasantly warm. A consolation from the cold.

Brown Leather stopped by her stomach, gun aimed directly at her face.

'Please...' she whispered. Weak, feeble. 'I want... I want to see.'

To her surprise, with the help of another, Brown Leather propped her on her knees.

Now, she knew, this was it.

Arabella looked skyward. Small flakes of snow descended and landed on her face, her hair, her hands. The flakes burned her skin and reminded her of the gentle pinches her mother gave her to lull her into a sleep after a bad nightmare.

Somewhere, off in the distance, was the moon, lurking behind the cushions of white above. She couldn't see it, but she knew it was there.

Like the wind.

Like the bullet that was fired from the 9mm a few inches behind her head.

Then the nightmare stopped and she fell asleep.

22

X

The clock was ticking.

Tick.

Tock.

Tick.

Tock.

Counting down the hours, minutes, seconds until they caught up with The Milkman and rescued Arabella.

By his estimates they were an hour behind. Two, max. A number shortened considerably thanks to his driving across the M25 and M20 on the way down to Kent. The short stretch of M26 had flashed past in a blur.

It had taken them a little under an hour to arrive

in Dover, at the small warehouse located by Alfie and the team a few miles west from the port. It was just after 2 a.m., and the weather had significantly worsened. The snow, combined with the freezing temperatures, were beginning to create hazardous situations, especially as they exchanged the safety of the motorways for the rural, untouched lanes of the Kentish countryside. When they pulled up on the outskirts of the warehouse, they found what appeared to be Kent Police's entire fleet of vehicles stationed on the side of the empty road, waiting. Almost everyone was inside their respective cars, sheltering from the elements.

Jake and Danika climbed out of the car and jogged towards the head of the convoy. Standing in front of an unmarked police car was a group of uniformed officers. Jake and Danika introduced themselves.

'PS Hansen,' the last officer to introduce himself said. 'I'm the operational firearms commander.'

'Good to meet you, sir,' Jake replied.

The OFC was the one responsible for implementing the strategy set by the Strategic Firearms Commander, who was sitting behind a desk somewhere. Hansen was the man on the ground who made sure everything went according to plan, and was responsible for resolving it if it didn't.

'We've been here for the past twenty minutes,' Hansen continued, his face white against the cold. 'We've positioned ourselves here so that they don't suspect us.'

'Here' was a hundred yards away from the industrial estate where the warehouse was situated. A small field, overgrown with weeds and shrubs and fast food detritus separated them. Clusters of silver birch trees lined the field sporadically, as though their original planters had got lazy and dropped handfuls of seed in a only a few places. To all intents and purposes the warehouse, and those around it, were uninhabited. There were no lights, no sounds of life, nothing.

But as the saying goes there was no knowing what was happening behind closed doors.

Not until they got close enough to find out.

'Have you confirmed any visuals, had any sightings?' Jake asked. He was beginning to feel the cold, and so he placed his hands in his trouser pockets and shuffled from one side to the other to keep himself warm.

'Nothing,' replied Hansen.

'Are they already here?'

Hansen shook his head. 'I sent one of the unmarked vehicles to do a recce earlier, and they found nothing.'

Strange, Jake thought. And the ticking grew louder.

Tick.

Tock.

Reverberating around his skull.

Reminding him of what was at stake.

The life of an innocent woman.

The potential lives of several dozen, hundred, thousand more.

'So what are we going to do?' Jake asked. The investigation was very much in Kent Police's hands, which meant that he and Danika had very little say in proceedings. Simply put, they were there to help, to watch, and in some respects, to learn.

Nothing like learning on the job.

But that didn't stop him from forcing their hand and doing everything he could to make sure they rescued Arabella.

'I'm giving it another ten minutes before we go in and find out what we're dealing with. Any longer than that, and we risk missing the opportunity.'

'As soon as we've sent in the AFOs, I'll give you guys access to look around,' Hansen finished.

'Thanks,' Jake replied, fighting off a yawn. 'Appreciate it. I'll speak with our team to see if they've got an update for us.'

They had nothing. All of a sudden they'd lost the vehicle on ANPR and CCTV around the M25. And they had no idea where it was going.

Now they were faced with the monumental challenge of finding it.

Like the blind leading the blind.

Jake fed back the news to PS Hansen.

'Fuck it,' he said, his decision made, 'we're going in now.'

And for the second time that evening, Jake watched a unit of twenty armed officers surround a warehouse, storm in, and efficiently secure it. The screams of 'Armed Police!' were still echoing around the factory floor by the time Jake and Danika entered. Fully dressed in their stab vests, they were joined by a team of ten uniformed officers. This time however, they were the first to enter.

The Milkman's warehouse was completely devoid of life. The structure itself was half the size of the one he and the team had rescued Anthony from, but it was still large enough to fit a 36-wheeler HGV inside. To his immediate right was a row of five-foot-tall lockers that looked like they'd been stolen from a gym's changing rooms. Beside them, in the corner, was a small mountain of buckets and mops, still wet, emanating a pungent stench that, fortunately, hadn't permeated the walls and reached outside. Running along the right-hand side of the building was a runway of sleeping bags and single mattresses, punctured and damaged from years of use. The rest of the warehouse was empty, save for a pyramid of spider trap boxes on the opposite side of the warehouse. One of the armed officers was in the middle of inspecting them. As soon as he lifted the lid open, he whistled, distracting everyone's attention.

Jake hurried over, his feet, and that of the uniformed officers, echoing around the space.

The pyramid was twice the size of Jake. Taller. Wider. Deeper. And each of the boxes was the same size as a car engine. The officer inspecting them reached inside and, slowly, tentatively, as if doing so suddenly would create chaos, he removed a set of women's clothes. A pink tank top. A thin white bra and matching underwear. A denim skirt.

Hundreds of articles of clothing, discarded, dirtied, stained with mud and what looked like blood.

Jake took a step back and allowed his mind to begin piecing it all together.

There was no doubt that this was the place The Milkman and his team were bringing the trafficked women across. Perhaps they were dumping them out the back of the lorry, forcing them to sleep on the floor, on the mattresses, enduring such squalid and inhumane conditions, relieving themselves in the buckets in the corner and being forced to clean after themselves. And the clothes were either their own or the outfits they were forced to wear if they wanted to be integrated into the societal dream they were promised.

'It makes me sick,' Danika reflected. 'How could anyone do this to other people? Make them live like this, treat them like this? It's disgusting.' A lump caught in her throat and she ran a finger through her hair. 'Excuse me,' she continued, 'I need a moment.'

It was the first sign of emotion that Jake had seen from her in all their years working together, and it unsettled him. Usually one not to show what she would call a weakness, she frequently smiled and ploughed through her difficulties. And he could only imagine the way she was feeling. Danika was much closer to the women's situations than anyone else in the room. Intrinsically linked by a desire to find better prospects, to find safety, refuge, a chance of a solid life. A Slovenian international herself, he knew that she'd experienced what it was like to move country, to be filled with hope and excitement at the new opportunities awaiting her, only to have them crushed by the opportunistic few. She'd struggled at first; failing to land a job, missing rent payments, almost finding herself on the streets. If it hadn't been for her chance meeting with her husband, who later introduced the route of becoming a police officer to her, he wondered whether she'd have been in a similar situation to Simona and the other women they were trying to protect.

And the other women they were too late in protecting.

The atmosphere in the van was frosty, desolate. Everyone was in a state of shock. Poor Arabella's death had been so sudden, so brutal, that they were all trying to process it. Perhaps it was because she was a woman, or perhaps it was because she hadn't deserved it. Their previous victims – Zeke, Jason, Leigh, and several others – had done something to warrant their extermination. They'd betrayed him, stolen from him, crossed the line some way or another. But with Arabella...

Her only mistake was trying to save herself.

And she was his first ever female victim – *their* first ever female victim.

But she was dead. What was done was done. And there was nothing they could do to change that.

'Pass me my phone,' The Milkman said, snapping his fingers at Tyrone beside him.

The henchman, shoulders almost as wide as the van itself, shimmied in the seat and reached down to the glove compartment where he retrieved Marek's burner phone, a Nokia 2310. His most reliable piece of machinery.

The Milkman snatched the device from Tyrone and, keeping one eye on the road and one eye on the screen, he thumbed his way through the address book. He stopped when he found the contact he was looking for.

The name in the address book read X.

He'd often wondered what the police or other investigating officers would think if they ever seized his phone and saw the contact. How they'd deduce and find X. Was it because he was a fan of the X-Men? Or his idol was a young Vin Diesel playing a special agent in a high-octane action thriller?

Neither.

Sadly, the reality was a lot more boring than that.

The name behind X was Charlie Hunter, a fishing boat owner who lived in the coastal town of Dover. For a small monthly retainer, he was kept on the books to help Marek and his team smuggle the girls into the country if their usual avenues failed or stumbled. Capable of carrying between ten and fifteen people across at a time, he was reliable, discreet and most importantly, he was aware of the consequences that would befall him if he no longer chose to toe the line.

Another nickname for him – a self appointed moniker, in fact – was The Pirate, because he was able to deliver the girls to several locations around the Kentish coast.

And in all instances, X marked the spot.

The Milkman dialled Charlie's number.

'Who's this?'

'It's me,' Marek replied. 'You awake?'

'I am now,' came the groggy response. 'I should've known you'd call. I had a feeling.'

'We need your help.'

'When?'

'Twenty minutes?'

They passed a sign on the motorway telling them that Dover Port was less than fifteen miles away.

'Twenty five,' The Pirate replied.

'Fine.'

'Where?'

'The usual place. X marks the spot.'

A pause. The Milkman sensed The Pirate was smiling down the phone.

'Of course… X marks the spot.'

23

Footsteps

Jake's phone vibrated against his leg. In his sleep deprived state, it took him a few seconds longer than usual to notice it. When he did, he glanced at the Caller ID and scurried away towards the warehouse's exit.

As he breached into the night air, he was sucker-punched by a fist of frost that instantly bit into his fingers and reached down to the bone.

'Hello?' he answered, trying to stop his teeth from chattering.

'Jake, it's Alfie. Where are you now?'

Jake looked around him. At the wall of darkness. At the trees that swayed gently in the wind. At the flecks of white paint descending gracefully from the sky. 'Just stepped out of the warehouse, mate. It's empty. There's no sign of them, except there are loads of women's clothes and sleeping bags all over the place. I think they keep the girls here for a—'

'Yeah, yeah, yeah, that's great,' Alfie interrupted, the urgency in his voice profound. 'We've got intelligence that suggests they're heading towards the cliffs.'

'Of Dover?'

Of course Dover, idiot. Where else?

Before Alfie had a chance to respond, Jake continued, 'How do you know? What intelligence?'

The sound of papers rustling reached down the phone. 'We've just got a trace and intercept on The Milkman's phone number. Now we can see precisely where they are and listen to all the calls they've made. And they just made one to someone ten minutes ago.'

'What makes you think they're going to the cliffs?'

'Because of what we found in Zeke's notebook. There are several mentions in emails and Zeke's shitty handwriting about Langdon and Crab Bay on the Cliffs of Dover. It's the place they sometimes dropped off some of the women if they couldn't get them across in the back of a lorry. There's also something about X marks the spot in there. Does that ring any bells?'

Jake considered it for a moment.

'Never heard of it. Except when I was a kid.'

Alfie dismissed the comment and continued, 'We're sending some more uniform down there now.

Not sure whether they'll make it in time, but you need to pass this information on to the SIO. You don't have much time left until they get there.'

'You think they're going to jump?' Jake asked.

Then heard the question in his head, realised how stupid it sounded.

'No,' Alfie replied, more calmly this time. 'We think they're going to try and flee the fucking country.'

Less than ten minutes later, Jake, Danika, and the rest of the Kent Police force were waiting on the Cliffs of Dover, shrouded in the anonymity of darkness amidst the quiet paths and trees that lined the cliff's edge.

The decision had been made, by Hansen and the Strategic Firearms Commander, to spread all the available units across the breadth of the cliffs, stretching from Dover Port all the way to St Margaret's Bay. In addition, an Airbus H135, a member of the National Police Air Service, was currently on standby in Redhill. As were a couple of boats from Kent Police's Marine Unit, ready to strike as soon as they spotted any sign of The Milkman's escape vessel.

Jake and Danika were at the base of the operation, hiding at the top level of the National Trust's gravelled car park. The site was home to a small cafe, a set of toilets, and an array of benches that looked out upon the English Channel. They were accompanied by two officers, one armed and one not, sitting in another unmarked car, communicating with them via radio. Each team was connected to the same frequency so that they could interact with one another and update everyone with the latest information.

The wait was monotonous, but the banter flying between the radio waves offered some light relief.

'My stomach's growling,' someone said.

'Your stomach's always growling,' replied another.

'Not nearly as much as his missus'll be growling by the time he gets home.'

That reminded him. Elizabeth. He'd forgotten to let her know that he wasn't coming home. Although if she hadn't worked it out by now then she never would. Still he pulled out his phone and sent her a brief message, telling her that he was alive, in Dover, and wouldn't be home until tomorrow afternoon. At the earliest. Hopefully the message wouldn't wake her nor Maisie. The last thing either of them needed was a rude awakening in the middle of the night.

'Everything all right?' Danika asked, nodding at his phone.

Jake glanced down at it and quickly slotted it in his pocket, as though he had something to hide. 'Just letting Elizabeth know where I am.'

'She's awake?'

'Hopefully not. But I didn't want her to worry. Better late than never. Have you spoken with Tony?'

Danika turned away and looked out of the window. The English Channel and the Cliffs of Dover were on the other side of the window, but inside the car, there was nowhere to escape the question.

'I tell him what he needs to know, when he needs to know it. Nothing more. Nothing less.'

Then, just as Jake was about to respond, Danika unbuckled her seatbelt and lowered the window.

'There! Look!'

She pointed, but Jake couldn't see through the thin blanket of snow that had fallen on the windscreen.

'What is it?' he asked.

'A black van. Headlights on. Just driving through to the end of the car park. They're… they're… they're not stopping.'

Without warning, they both leapt out of the car – grabbing their things in the process – and signalled to the officers accompanying them. Jake whispered into the radio.

'Visual sighted of a black van breaking through the barrier at the end of the National Trust car park, currently making its way along the public footpath on the edge of the cliff. Heading north. Approximately twenty miles an hour.'

Then the two men clambered out of the car with them, gear in hand, game faces on. But Danika was already off ahead of them, sprinting across the stones towards the footpath.

Jake and the two officers followed.

The chase was on.

Ten minutes. That was all they needed to get down

there. And then they'd have done it. Fled the country, where they could lie low for a while and then return until the proverbial dust had settled.

Ten minutes to offload, climb down the steps at Langdon Bay where X marked the spot, hop into the freezing water and climb aboard The Pirate's ship.

Ten minutes, allowing for the treacherous conditions.

The van jostled and shook as they tore through the wooden gate and traversed the uneven and unmade public footpath. The surface was undulating, riddled with potholes, but they didn't bother Marek. This wasn't his first rodeo, nor was it his first time arriving here in the middle of the night. Except, in the last circumstances, he was picking up women, rather than dropping them off.

'How's she doing?' Marek asked as he glanced in the rear-view mirror.

Boris's oversized face occupied most of it. He turned, shook Clarissa, and replied, 'Still gone. I don't know what you did to her, but it's not natural for her to be out for this long.'

'Check her pulse. Make sure she's alive.'

Anthony Sharman still owed him a debt, and if that debt was dead, then Marek was going to be one unhappy man. He just hoped he hadn't shot the wrong girl.

'She's breathing, and I can feel her pulse.'

Marek exhaled deeply. Best news he'd heard all night. Clarissa was his best chance at making a profit, of covering the losses he'd incurred by putting his faith in Anthony and Zeke. Not only was she a beautiful girl, but she was a virgin to the world of dancing and performing deeds for money. For that, she would fetch a higher price and he could almost hear the sound of paper being counted, of the sweet smell of cash climbing through his nostrils.

A minute later, after driving cautiously through the wet and slippery terrain, they arrived at the ledge that led down to Langdon Bay. Marek killed the car, left the keys in the ignition and hopped out. The sky was a dense, dark grey, and cast an eerie, ominous glow over them. The snow was coming down in droves, and they were being battered by the winds, assaulting them from the south.

Marek hurried to the back of the van with Boris, opened it, and pulled Clarissa out by her feet. Her body was like a dead weight, and she'd need at least two people to carry her.

As he and Boris calculated a way to transport her, Marek signalled to the others to grab the rest of their things from the back. The latest shipment of drugs. The small gym bags containing their emergency stash of cash. And anything else that could be of benefit to them as they started a brief life on the continent.

As soon as they were done, he gave them the order to torch the vehicle.

Nodding, Herman, a grey brute of a man, raced to the front, produced a tube from the glove compartment, and slotted it into the petrol cap. He sucked and sucked until eventually the petrol came out of the tube. Then he started dousing the vehicle in the fluid. Once everything was covered in the flammable liquid, Herman whipped out a lighter and threw it into the back. Despite the harsh winds and the flurry of snowfall, the vehicle ignited with ease, and within seconds a ball of fire blistered the metal and exterminated everything inside.

'Come on!' Marek called, peering over the edge of the cliff. Two white lights floated furiously in the water several hundred feet below. 'The Pirate's here. Go, go, go.'

By his estimations, they were three minutes down, and had another seven minutes to go. Seven minutes to navigate the wet and slippery steps.

Easy.

That was, until he heard the faintest sound of footsteps behind him.

He turned to see four individuals standing a few metres away. One of them pointing a firearm at him, aimed directly at his centre mass.

24

Trigger Finger

Jake was unsure precisely what it was that alerted
The Milkman to their presence. Their feet, muffled
by the layer of snow now resting on the paths and
pieces of gravel? Their breathing, hurried and
exasperated in the cold? Or perhaps it was pure
chance, a sixth sense, the heightened sense of
paranoia you get when you're doing something you
know you shouldn't.

Either way, The Milkman noticed them too soon,
and now there was nearly a twenty metre gap
between them. With a deadly obstacle in the way.

By now, the black Transit van had erupted into a
giant ball of fire, and bursts of flames were climbing
out of the windows and dancing in the air. The thing

about it that concerned Jake the most, however, was not the obvious threat of catching fire and burning to death: it was in fact the fierce light that was almost blinding him, as if he was staring into the sun.

Through half-closed eyes, Jake counted six individuals. Five men, one woman. Arabella. In The Milkman's arms. Unconscious. Or, worse, dead. And they were trying to dispose of her by either dropping her down the face of the cliff or throwing her body overboard as soon as they'd made some headway into the Channel.

'Put your hands in the air!' the armed officer screamed, his voice barely audible over the roaring sound of the blaze beside them.

The Milkman reacted first.

He rotated slowly, keeping Arabella in his arms. And in doing so, the other man holding her legs was forced to move in tandem with The Milkman. As the gang member circled round, his foot caught on a dip in the Earth, dropped Arabella's feet to the ground, and stumbled over the side of the cliff. In a flash, he was gone, somersaulting two hundred feet down to the ground.

Nobody heard his screams.

Nobody heard the noise of his body on impact.

As though he'd never even been there.

Jake's eyes widened as he stared at the place the gang member had just been, caught in a moment of shock. But The Milkman remained unfazed, undeterred. And so did the armed officer.

Both individuals were on high alert, senses finely tuned to their surroundings. As for Jake,

Danika, and the uniformed officer whose name he didn't know, they were pointless. There was nothing they could, and their attendance made no difference to the outcome.

And then it all changed.

The Milkman, slowly, calmly, as though he had nothing to worry about, reached into his back pocket and pulled a gun out. Placed it delicately against Arabella's temple, as though doing so harder would inflict damage upon her.

Now the dynamic had changed.

They'd gone from one gun, to two. And as Jake surveyed the other gang members crouching behind The Milkman, halfway down the steps, he hoped they weren't about to add any more to the mix.

'Put the gun down and raise your hands in the air!' the armed officer bellowed. This time his voice was picked up by the wind.

The radio in Jake's hand bleated. The rest of Kent police confirming their position, notifying him that they were two minutes out.

'Received,' Jake whispered into the handset. 'Be aware the suspect has a gun against the victim's head. Repeat, suspect in possession of a firearm. One body over the edge of the cliff. Approach with extreme caution.'

'Received, over.'

And then everything went silent again.

In the short time he'd been on the radio, the weather had deteriorated. The wind had picked up. The clouds had thickened and darkened, and the snow was pelting him in the face. Despite the

169

numbness seeping through his bones, the snowflakes felt as though someone was rubbing a Brillo pad over his skin.

'Put the fucking gun down, mate!' The armed officer took a step forward, keeping the SIG Carbine trained on The Milkman.

'Don't get any closer,' The Milkman replied.

The officer ignored him and took another step. Everyone else followed. Bridging the gap between them slowly.

'It's over!' someone called. 'Let her go!'

Jake was surprised to learn he was the one responsible for the outburst. His lips were moving faster than his brain. And he wondered whether he was experiencing some sort of mental brain freeze.

'We've got you surrounded,' Jake continued, inching closer with each word. 'There's nowhere left to run.'

'This can be very easy for you if you put the gun down and let us go.' The Milkman flicked a clump of snow from his eye with a shake of the head. 'No one has to get hurt.'

Somehow, Jake didn't believe that. The Milkman had already shown that he was willing to hurt and kill anyone that got in his way. What difference did four police officers make?

'Just let her go, put the gun down,' the armed officer said. 'Otherwise I will be forced to shoot.'

This was useless. They were getting nowhere. They were out of their depth.

But then everything changed.

Shouts and commotion erupted from the gang

members hiding behind The Milkman. They pointed, alerting their crime boss to the onslaught of police officers and vehicles bounding towards them across the horizon, headlights cutting through the undulating surfaces like a scythe through paper.

As soon as he saw the reinforcements, The Milkman panicked.

Frantically, he threw Arabella to the ground and held the gun to his chin, pointed upwards. The movement was so smooth, so calculated it suggested he'd done it before. But there was something about this situation that concluded The Milkman wasn't joking, wasn't messing about.

'I'm not going to prison. I'm not fucking going! You'll never fucking get me in a cell!'

The armed officer screamed at the man to lower the weapon, to come to his senses and put the fucking thing down before he did anything stupid.

Jake joined in.

Danika joined in.

Their screams, along with the roaring fire, the approaching helicopter way off in the distance, the deafening wind, all created a cacophony of sound that disorientated and petrified.

Jake stood frozen to the spot, paralysed by fear. He felt the onset of another anxiety attack coming, calling out to him, screaming his name as it rapidly arrived. But he stifled it and dismissed it.

There were bigger things to worry about.

Like the fact that one squeeze of the trigger was all it would take to —

25

Arabella

The crack of the bullet whipped around the cliffs, immediately rendering everything still, quiet.

Jake's eyes remained open throughout. He was expecting to see a plume of blood explode from above The Milkman's head, a flower of blood to spawn on his chest and slowly seep through his leather jacket. He was expecting to see the hardened criminal collapse to the ground and slowly die on the snow.

The reality was different.

The Milkman was still standing, gun in hand, pointed at his chin. But his face was bleeding. The bullet had travelled through his lip, rupturing the skin and potentially his gums, and burst a hole through the left side of his nose.

Jake looked down to see Arabella was awake, clinging to The Milkman's legs, clawing at his groin, beating his stomach.

In the moments before the gunshot, she'd awoken and assaulted him. The sudden, unanticipated attack had knocked the gun from against The Milkman's chin, and as he'd fired it, the bullet missed all the vital organs.

He was alive. Very much alive.

And Jake, Danika, the armed officer and the uniformed officer made no hesitation in making sure it stayed that way.

Within an instant, all four of them were sprinting towards The Milkman, Jake finding himself at the front of the pack.

He was first to arrive and immediately rugby tackled the criminal to the floor. His body was soft, helped by the comfort of the brown leather jacket. The Milkman fought for the weapon, but his grip was weak, and Jake discard it with ease, throwing it a few feet away towards the burning wreckage. While he was tussling with The Milkman, Danika and the uniformed officer raced towards the gang members who were trying to escape down the steps. They made it as far as the second before being felled and cuffed.

Jake gasped for breath as he struggled to his feet. As he reached down to grab The Milkman and place a set of handcuffs around his wrist, the armed officer appeared.

'I'll deal with this,' he said, 'you deal with her.'

He gave a quick nod towards Arabella, but it was unnecessary; Jake was already on his feet.

His shoes – the loafers he'd laboured indecisively over one weekend in the town centre – slipped on the snow, and he landed awkwardly on his shoulder. Grimacing away the pain, with a face full of snow and dirt, he clambered up.

Sitting there, legs propped against her chest, head cowered down into her knees, sobbing uncontrollably, was Arabella.

'It's OK,' Jake told her as he placed a hand on her back. 'Everything's going to be OK. You're safe now.'

She didn't respond.

'Come on, let's get you up. We'll get you somewhere warm.'

At that moment, the rest of Kent Police arrived and quickly sealed the scene. A little too late, but the job was done.

'You coming?' Jake asked, as though presenting her with the illusion of choice would make her ordeal any better.

And then she lifted her head.

And Jake realised it wasn't Arabella at all.

That he'd assumed it was the wrong girl all along.

Instead it was Clarissa, Anthony's sister. Her hand badly bruised and swollen. *Which explains the vice on the floor.*

Which meant that Arabella was still out there somewhere.

174

26

No Answer

Marek Novak, human trafficker and criminal, wanted in several countries by a handful of law enforcement officers, was sitting opposite him, leaning against the wall, attention focused elsewhere. It was just gone noon, and after the events of the early morning, Marek had been taken to the nearest hospital where he was treated for his injuries. In the eyes of medical professionals, they weren't nearly as bad as those that Anthony and Clarissa had sustained. After a quick surgery, he was released, his nose and lips bandaged and stitched. Aside from looking like he'd been slightly mauled by a tiger, he was declared fit for interview. In the time that he was being treated, some of the members of Croydon CID had started interviewing Marek's gang members. But they weren't budging, remaining stoic and silent.

Meanwhile Jake and DC Helen Spencer had spent the past few hours preparing for the big one. Marek's interview. By now, all the officers that had clocked in were fresh-faced and fully rested. Except for Jake. Awake for nearly twenty-four hours and beginning to feel the effect of sleep deprivation and lethargy, he was just about getting by thanks to a mixture of coffee and energy drinks. This was his first ever interview since joining the team, and it was the main reason he'd stayed put for so long, despite Payne and Carmichael's protestations for him to go home. Jake wanted to finish the job, see it through to the end. And find Arabella before he even thought about going anywhere.

Twelve hours had passed since she'd disappeared, and they were still no closer to finding her. Jake hoped, however marginal and unlikely it was, that Marek would give them the information they needed.

'It'll be difficult, but not impossible,' Helen had said to him while they prepared, with a particular spring in her step, as if she'd either got laid the night before or had had a really good night's sleep. Right before they'd entered the interview room, she'd stopped and said, 'For the time being, let me lead. I'll bring you in if necessary, OK? Best way to learn is on the job, eh?'

She'd flashed him a wink but Jake could only reply with a wry, half-arsed smile. If he didn't have to hear that phrase ever again, it wouldn't be the worst thing to happen today.

Sitting alongside Marek was his solicitor, a young woman who wore a set of bags under her eyes that matched her hair colour. She was caught between the age of caring about them enough so as to cover them with make-up, but not caring about them so much that her face was caked in it. She seemed, peculiarly, to wear them as a badge of honour, as if they were proof of the amount of hard work she put in for her job.

Once everyone was settled, Helen reached across the desk and pressed *Play* on the recorder. A small buzzer sounded, and Jake's eyes fell away from the device and landed on Marek. The man remained indignant.

'Marek, we'd like to begin by asking you a few questions in relation to the death of Zeke Harrison, on the night of the fifth of December,' Helen said.

Marek remained unperturbed.

'Where were you on the night of the fifth?'

Nothing. Silence.

'Who were you with?'

Still nothing.

'What's your relationship with Zeke Harrison?'

While Helen launched a barrage of questions at Marek – how did you know Zeke? How long have you worked together? – Jake studied and surveyed the man's reactions, the movements in his face as he ignored everything that came his way. The body language, the signs and symbols suggesting he wanted to answer a question, but something in his deep-seated sense of self-preservation prohibited him from doing so.

Slowly but surely, as the relentless assault of accusations and information continued, they were breaking down the barriers and getting closer to a response, an outburst of emotion, a criminal stuck in catharsis.

And Jake was ready for it when it came.

'Why did you kill Zeke, Marek?' Helen continued. Her fingers spun the white plastic cup on the desk, a casual display of muscle memory from how frequently she played with her Coke cans in meetings. 'We've got CCTV footage of the van you torched driving to and from Eloquence on the night of the fifth. We've then got the same vehicle heading from the club to the Beddington Farmlands, where Zeke was later murdered. And then, shortly after, the vehicle was seen visiting Anthony Sharman's house. It was there for a little bit and then it made a detour to another club owned by Zeke Harrison. You found Anthony Sharman in that club, didn't you? And then you threw him into the back of the van.' Spencer paused a moment. A lot of this was news to Jake. Alfie *really* had been busy in the past forty-eight hours. 'We also found several boot prints at the crime scene, as well as DNA residue on Zeke Harrison's body and the murder weapon. When we examine it, are we going to find your fingerprints, is that murder weapon going to be directly linked to you, Marek? What about the car? Did you think that burning it would destroy any evidence? Because it won't. We'll find everything we need to in there.'

Still nothing.

Marek's chest continued to rise and fall steadily. Up, down, up, down. A certain rhythm to it. As though last night had never happened, that his face wasn't badly mauled and disfigured.

'Why'd you kill him, Marek?' Jake asked before he could catch himself. He didn't mean to step out of turn, but he was growing increasingly impatient, and he wanted answers. Information. Now.

As soon as Jake finished the question, Marek's head turned, and his dark, evil eyes, landed on Jake.

'He talks...' Marek noted, his words slurred by the missing chunk and stitches in his lip.

He can do a lot more than that.

Going against their agreed plan, Jake continued. 'Was it personal?'

'In my line of work it's never personal. Just business. Pure and simple.'

'Did Zeke owe you money?'

'Money he couldn't pay. That's not my fault.'

'Let me guess, it's not your fault he's dead, either?'

Marek's eyes remained glued to Jake's. 'The only thing I'm guilty of is trusting him and believing that he could pay what he owed.'

'And when he couldn't you passed the debt on to Anthony...'

'Anthony was next in line to inherit the debt. It was only natural.'

'And when Anthony couldn't come up with the money?' Helen interrupted. 'What were you going to do then? What were you going to do with him?'

Marek's head turned ominously towards her, as though he were planning on ways to leap over the table and strangle her. After he'd sussed her out for a bit, he slowly turned back to Jake, a look of contempt expressed clearly on his face.

When Marek didn't answer Helen's question, Jake understood the reason. Before him was a man who had no respect for women. None. The fact he made a living by extorting them and trafficking them was testament to that. And the cherry on the cake was his defiance in the face of his colleague's questions.

Piece of shit, Jake thought, censoring himself when there were far worse words he could have used to describe the despicable human being opposite him. After realising Marek wasn't going to answer anything posed to him by Helen, he repeated the question.

'If we hadn't arrived when we did, was Anthony Sharman going to die last night?'

For a long while, nobody said anything and the room fell still, silent, devoid of life. Even the humming from the air conditioning overhead seemed to stop.

Until Marek nodded.

'The other night,' Marek started, 'Zeke was hugged by death's embrace. Anthony almost experienced what that was like, but he was fortunate enough to escape. Who knows, maybe he won't be so lucky in the future. The same with his sister.'

'Is that a threat?'

Marek shook his head. 'That man has many

enemies, some far greater than me. It's only a matter of time before someone gets him good.'

'And what about Arabella – where is she? What have you done with her?' Helen asked, stepping in again. Jake resented her for interrupting the flow of things, but he understood her reasons.

'I don't answer questions from an inferior,' Marek said. 'I won't answer any more.'

'Please,' Jake said, glad they were finally getting to the most important part of the interview. 'Arabella…where is she?'

'Somewhere.'

'Is she alive?'

No answer.

'Have you killed her?'

Still no answer.

'Where's the body, Marek?'

Marek tilted forward a fraction, drawing himself closer to the microphone. 'No… comment…'

27

Good People

Later that afternoon, the beast from the east had headed west, and the carpets of snow that stretched across the countryside, undisturbed by civilisation and the elements, were beginning to melt. The surrounding scenery was quiet, still, serene. It was perhaps the most beautiful part of the country Jake had ever seen – a remote stretch of tarmac surrounded by woodlands and fields in the bowels of the Surrey Hills.

It was a shame then that it was destroyed by the four police vehicles, three forensics vans, army of news reporters and white forensic tent.

Arabella – or Natalie, as Jake later discovered was her real name – had been discovered by a jogger, a keen marathon runner in his thirties who wasn't going to let a little bit of snow ruin his training programme.

The man had left in the afternoon, after the snow had started to thaw, and along his usual route, he'd spotted a dead deer in the middle of the road. Upon closer inspection, he'd noticed a disturbance in the field, realised it was a dead body, and then called the police. Within minutes, the emergency responders arrived, cordoned off the stretch of road, and erected the forensic tent to protect her body from the elements.

The cause of death was obvious. Gunshot wound. To the back of the head. A merciless killing. A *coward's* killing.

Jake was filled with anger and despair. He'd tried to protect her, find her, save her. But it had been for nothing. She'd died unnecessarily.

The only consolation was that it had been over quickly for her – no drawn-out suffering, no prolonged exposure to immeasurable pain.

Bang. Dead.

Nice and clean, nice and simple.

He told himself Arabella's alternative – a lifetime of rape and torture, of harassment and brutality, of perpetual fear and poverty – was perhaps far worse than the fate she'd met. And it was far better than the death's embrace that could have killed her.

'You all right?' Danika asked, placing a hand on his shoulder. He hadn't realised it, but he'd been staring into the white tent, the foreground melting into the background like a Bob Ross painting. Except this time there were no happy clouds, no happy little accidents. Just death and disappointment.

'Fine,' he lied. 'It's a shame it happened like this. Shame it happened at all.'

Danika moved her hand to the top of his back, gave a gentle squeeze.

'You can't save them all,' she told him. 'It's shit, I know. But like the guv said, it's always the good people that suffer the most.'

Jake feigned a smile.

Wasn't that the truth.

28

IOU

Jake knocked on DCI Payne's door and entered without waiting. Already in the room was Danika, and the sight of her filled him with a dark premonition, a knot in his stomach.

In the past twenty-four hours, Arabella's body had been removed from the crime scene, inspected by the pathologist, and cleared for her parents to visit. Clarissa had been admitted to hospital and was being treated for severe injuries to her hand and wrist, concussion and an infection she'd picked up while lying face down on the floor of the factory. Her injuries were minor compared to the mental toll the events of that night would have on her. But Jake was optimistic that, with a little help from professionals, she'd make a quick recovery. Anthony, on the other hand, was in intensive care, the damage sustained to his skull having caused a bleed on the brain, and he was now fighting for his life. It wasn't know when or if he would wake up. Meanwhile Marek Novak and the remaining members of his gang were charged with murder, attempt murder, human trafficking and GBH, along with a litany of other charges, and were currently on their way to a handful of prison cells.

'All things considered,' DCI Payne began, setting his mug of tea on his desk, 'I'd say it's been a success. And it's not often I admit I'm wrong, Tanner, but in this instance I was. You were right about Zeke's secrets.'

Jake felt disbelief. It was the first time he'd received any form of praise from his senior officer, and he didn't know quite how to take it. Perhaps the man was finally beginning to change and recognise him for the good, hard-working detective he was.

'Just doing my job, guv,' he said, shrugging, attempting to downplay his role in the outcome of the investigation.

'But...'

Oh no. There was a but. Why was there always a but?

'...therein lies the problem,' Payne continued. He prodded his finger in his ear and wiggled it about. When he removed it, he wiped it clean between his other fingers and placed his hands on the desk, expression blank, as though the personal hygiene check hadn't happened. 'I've been a bit concerned, as have other members of the team, about your behaviour, both of you.'

'*Our* behaviour?'

'Your attitude.' Payne's eyes met Jake's. They were cold, unnerving, but Jake resolved himself not to break contact. 'The way you went about things could have been handled better. The way you disrespected myself, DI Carmichael, DS Coker, and the rest of the team. It doesn't mean to say you're—'

'I'm sorry, guv,' Jake said, holding his hand in the air. 'But I disagree with that. We were overlooked at every turn. We came to you about the human trafficking, the fact Zeke wasn't the hero you thought he was, and you disregarded it. It wasn't until Anthony Sharman almost died and one of his workers was kidnapped that you finally paid attention.'

'We have our hypotheses for a reason. I'm the one in charge of making them and I say we stick to them.'

'Until someone else from the team points out what we already had, and then they take all the credit for it…'

'Not at all, and I find the insinuation abhorrent.' Payne paused and turned his attention to Danika. Perhaps he was expecting an easier ride with her. 'This is in no way a reflection of your abilities as detectives – you're both very good, and you've proven that. You both have exceptional qualities and careers ahead of you. But—'

Another but. This was going to be bad.

'But, for the time being, I think it's in all our interests if we distance ourselves from one another. There are two positions available in Guildford, so I'm seconding you to Surrey Police.' Payne picked his ears again, this time with the other hand. 'The wheels have been set in motion on my end. It'll take a while to process, but I think you'll be much better suited to working down there. There's plenty more breathing space to learn, and I have no doubt that you'll both flourish. I've given you both glowing reviews and recommendations. I'm sorry it's come to this, but as things stand, they're just not going to work out.'

Jake fell silent. The knot in his stomach wrapped itself around his organs and tightened. And tightened. And tightened. Until it made him feel sick and the rest of his body ache.

He was being chucked out of the team, disregarded, thrown away. Used and abused. They'd got him to help solve the case for them, and now they were abandoning him, like a toy growing out of favour with a child.

'Is that all?' Jake asked. 'I've got things to be getting on with.'

He couldn't deny that he was hurt, and he hoped that it came across in the way he spoke. If Payne showed any sign of remorse or anguish about the decision, he didn't show it.

Which told Jake all he needed to know.

'There is one more thing,' Payne began.

'Yeah?'

'I've always made it a thing – you might have seen it around the place or heard of it mentioned in the office – where the top detective working on a case gets a free coffee of their choice from me. Because you were both so excellent, I'd like to buy you both one.'

What? A free coffee and a sacking, lucky us! The prick.

Jake inhaled deeply, composed himself and then climbed out of the chair. He wasn't ready to be mocked and belittled like that. 'I'll pass, thanks,' he said as he started towards the door. 'But if you're really set on it, then you can write me an IOU.'

ALSO BY JACK PROBYN
The Jake Tanner Crime Thriller series:

THE CONSPIRACY:

A small jeweller's is raided in Guildford High Street and leaves police chasing their tails. Reports suggest that it's The Crimsons, an organised crime group the police have been hunting for years. When the shop owner is kidnapped and a spiked collar is attached to her neck, Jake learns one of his own is involved – a police officer. As Jake follows the group on a wild goose chase, he questions everything he knows about his team. Who can he trust? And is he prepared to find out?

THE COMMUNITY:

A couple with a nefarious secret are brutally murdered in their London art gallery. Their bodies cleaned. Their limbs dismembered. And the word LIAR inscribed on the woman's chest. For Jake Tanner it soon becomes apparent this is not a revenge killing. There's a serial killer loose on the streets of Stratford. And the only thing connecting the victims is their name: Jessica. Jake's pushed to his mental limits as he uncovers The Community, an online forum for singles and couples to meet. But there's just one problem: the killer's been waiting for him... and he's hungry for his next kill.

THE CONFESSION:
DC Jake Tanner thought he'd put the turmoil of the case that nearly killed him behind him. He was wrong. When Danny Cipriano's body is discovered buried in a concrete tomb, Jake's wounds are reopened. But one thing quickly becomes clear. The former leader of The Crimsons knew too much. And somebody wanted him silenced. For good. The only problem is, Jake knows who.

THE
CONSPIRACY

Turn over to read the first two chapters…

CHAPTER 1

PLAY DIRTY

SIX MONTHS AGO

Two years had passed since the world's media had last uttered their name. In that time, they'd been forgotten, disregarded and pushed to the bottom of the history books – more importantly, pushed to the bottom of the nation's police forces' unsolved case files. Where they should be.

There was a reason they were the best in the business and had already taken home more than two million pounds' worth of jewellery and money from their previous four heists. Their methods methodical, their planning meticulous. And with a certain amount of help from friends in high places, they were almost untouchable.

With each heist the pressure and risk grew exponentially, and every possible outcome had to be accounted for. And in the past it had – except in their last heist. Cock-up from start to finish. Oxford, 2006, HSBC bank on the high street, 9 a.m. Charge in, siege the place, force everyone into the centre of the room and destroy any and all means of communication, then pilfer the contents of the safes and ATM machines until their gym bags were brimming with sweet, sweet paper. Easy. At least it should have been.

The one thing they hadn't planned for was what they liked to call in the business a Good Samaritan: someone dumb enough and brave enough to stand in the way of sub-machine guns and shotguns and defend the bank until the police arrived. The name of that individual would forever be etched in their memories, including the minute details of his face. Not because he was instantly recognisable or because they all had photographic memories – far from it – but because the man had instantly earned himself some notoriety. Following the event, and the subsequent arrest of their former leader, the media had a hard-on for the Good Samaritan and gave him more airtime than they should have – far more than he deserved.

What the Good Samaritan was doing now, nobody knew, but they'd each resolved to make sure nothing like that happened again.

Next time would be different. Next time they would set the world alight and make sure their names were burnt into the retinas of anyone who saw them or dared cross them. They wanted to go rogue. Off the books. Off the radar. To commit the worst robbery ever seen and be immortalised by the media coverage that had followed them throughout their nine-year career. And they were going to make it exceptional.

It was time to forget the rules and play dirty.

CHAPTER 2

MEAN STREETS

SIX MONTHS LATER: JUNE, 2009

Jake Tanner had never been fond of first days. As far back as he could remember, they were always filled with awkwardness, facetious grins, overbearing smiles and greetings, and a solid case of nervy runs. But the one thing that stung him badly was shyness. The first day of school where you didn't know anyone in the playground and all the rest of the kids seemed to have made lifelong friends already. The first day of university where you were a day late to freshers' week because you were respecting the anniversary of your father's death, and everyone was beginning to get on like a student kitchen fire and build lasting relationships.

And today was no different: the first day of a new job, a new start to his professional career as a detective constable. New names, new faces, new personalities.

The sun beat down on the windshield of Jake's Mini Austin Cooper; he was barely able to fit into it, but it was his pride and joy nonetheless. The air conditioning was beat – the latest in the long list of repairs the car required – and the windows were having little effect against the monstrous and offensive heat that opened his pores and covered his body in a thin veil of sweat. The world outside the car was still – the trees, bushes on the side of the road, even the air. So far so good.

Jake glanced down at the satnav, wiping a layer of liquid from his top lip. *In a hundred yards, please turn right.* Easy enough. But if he needed a reminder, the sign bearing the words MOUNT BROWNE, SURREY POLICE he saw a few seconds later did its job. He slowed, turned and idled the car past a row of detached properties, his eyes searching for the correct entrance. There was no mistaking it. At the end of the road was an even bigger sign than the first. Between the two lanes sat a booth that reminded him of the ones at Dartford Crossing that he and his family used to drive past on their summer holidays to the Norfolk coast – the only time of year when his dad was allowed time off from work.

He rolled the car to the booth, held his warrant

card beneath the digital scanner and waited for the bar to lift, granting him access.

While the internal systems of the scanner worked quietly in the background, cross-referencing his face and his data with the police force's databases, he tilted forward and stared into the camera lens aimed directly at him. He thought about smiling childishly but suppressed the thought, remembering his place and where he was. Nerves did funny things to people.

Shortly after, the bar lifted and Jake drove up the steep incline towards the headquarters of Surrey Police, ignoring the agony of the engine running at five thousand revs in second gear. As he climbed over the lip of the hill, the knot in his stomach tightened, forcing pressure on his abdomen. He manoeuvred his way into the nearest parking space he could find: at the opposite end of the car park. It was only 7:50 a.m. and already the entire force was making him look bad.

He wasn't sure he could even plead innocence of it being his first day.

Mount Browne was a vast building and looked as though it had once been a stately mansion in a former life, a host for aristocracy and the wealthy, with its eaves, vaulted walls and several chimneys dotted along the roof. Now, however, it had been transformed into the hub of a vibrant and buzzing police force, the home of one of Surrey Police's satellite Major Crime Team divisions. The brick was a combination of black, brown and red, and stood front and centre, proud, against the backdrop of paradise green and sky blue.

With nothing but his backpack – which contained a packed lunch his wife Elizabeth had made for him and a reusable plastic bottle filled with water in anticipation of the heat – along with his phone, wallet and keys, Jake climbed a small flight of steps and entered the foyer. Inside he looked for signs of someone waiting for him, like he was stepping out of the arrivals lounge at Heathrow. There was nothing of the sort. Instead he was welcomed by an unenthused member of staff sitting behind the front desk at the far end of the entrance. A pen chained to the surface dangled over the edge, and a few police leaflets were fanned across the surface.

'Morning,' Jake said, feigning an excitable, I'm-so-happy-to-be-here smile. In reality that would only be genuine when the stomach cramps left him.

'Name?'

'Temporary Detective Constable Jake Tanner,' he said. 'Here to meet with DCI Nicki Pemberton.'

Jake removed his warrant card from his pocket and flashed it in the man's face, who immediately dismissed it and reached for a clipboard and slid it across the desk's surface.

'Sign in.'

Jake did as he was told and scribbled his name, rank and sign-in time on the sheet. Passing it back to the reception officer, he asked, 'Is there a coffee machine anywhere?'

The man grunted and pointed to Jake's right. Then he leant over the arm of his chair, disappearing beneath the desk and returned a moment later with a polystyrene cup. 'Put it in the bin when you're finished. Nicki will be down in a few minutes. You can wait over by the seats.'

Jake thanked him and moved over to the coffee machine. *Smart one, Jake. Have a natural laxative – that'll make you feel better.* He prodded the button for a latte and waited. As the steaming milk filled the cup, Jake read from the dozens of leaflets dangling from the corkboard on the wall. 'An Introduction to Your Rights'. 'So, You've Been Arrested'. 'How to Report a Crime'. 'How to Report a Police Officer'. Jake had read them all. Back to back. Cover to cover. Police training 101. But there was only so much you could learn from a manual, and there was no substitution for experience.

Once the coffee machine finished, Jake found himself a seat on a small armchair so old and dirty that when he sat down, a plume of dust billowed in the air. Fighting to keep his dust-induced sneeze down, he took a sip of the coffee and instantly wished he hadn't — it was bitter, too hot and made him gag. But it was enough to perk him up in the morning, even if it was going to haunt him in a few hours' time after the contents had mades its way through his stomach.

Jake bent forward to place the cup on a wooden

table in front of him that looked older than the building. He'd seen that type before and, for a moment, wondered whether all police stations shared the same coffee tables as those commonly found at doctors' surgeries – whether the public services budget extended as far as differentiating any of them. He didn't think it likely.

Someone called his name from behind, distracting him from his thoughts.

'DC Tanner.'

He flinched, almost knocking the cup to the floor, then composed himself before rising from the chair.

DCI Pemberton, a slim, experienced-looking woman with a lob haircut, stood with her hand extended. She was dressed in a full suit with trousers and a look on her face that told him even though she was happy to see him, he'd already taken too long in addressing her. Jake, in a frantic rush, as if he'd just locked eyes with a celebrity, wiped his hand on his trousers and took hers. With his other hand, he brushed his black-and-grey-striped tie down, centred it and pushed it deeper into his collar.

'Thank you for joining us,' Pemberton said. Her grip was powerful and firm, and she spoke with a certain authority he hadn't heard in a while.

'Thanks for having me as part of the team. I hope to learn a lot, and hopefully I can be of some assistance!'

'From what I hear, you already are. I've heard some exciting things about you. You travelled far this morning?'

He shrugged. 'Only Croydon.'

'Park all right?'

'Just about. And I thought I was here early this morning.'

Pemberton's gaze turned towards the building's entrance and then back to Jake. 'It's a free-for-all in the mornings. You should see the amount of fights that have broken out. We don't have designated spaces, but having said that, if you park in mine, I can assure you that your days with us will definitely be numbered.'

A P45 threat within the first minute. Well done, Jake. At this rate you'll be gone by lunchtime.

'Good coffee?' Pemberton asked.

Jake glanced over his shoulder at the bead of brown liquid abseiling down the length of the cup. 'Yeah, it was nice, thanks.' He rubbed his cheek, massaging his fingers over the small scar that prohibited any facial hair from growing around it.

Pemberton smirked, drawing Jake's eyes to her mouth and then down to her shirt collar covered in make-up residue. 'You're a superb liar,' she told him. 'You should fit in fine here. Come on – I'll take you up and show you to the rest of the team.'

The rest of the team. The cliques at school. The university accommodation where all the bonds had already been formed.

Pemberton started off towards a set of double doors at the back of the lobby. Jake shot one last look at the cup of coffee, checked he hadn't left anything else behind and followed. At the door, Pemberton scanned her card, and they both waited until a green light flashed above the reader.

Then she led Jake through a myriad of corridors and offices until they eventually stopped by a lift at the back of the building. Pemberton pressed the button, then, once inside, chose the fourth floor. Jake stood slightly behind her, his head craning at the red bar above the doors that moved from left to right as they climbed the building.

A surprise yawn attacked him and broke free, stretching his mouth wide open and filling his brain with oxygen. He threw his hand over his mouth.

'Boring you already?' Pemberton asked with a smile that put him at ease a little.

'Not at all. Hardly slept last night.'

'Nerves?'

That and everything else going on.

'The opposite.'

'I think you'll find Surrey's a little calmer than the mean streets of London. We don't have that much going on.'

Jake disagreed. 'There's *always* something going on.'

ABOUT JACK PROBYN

Jack Probyn hasn't experienced the world. He's never even owned a pet. But he'd like to; there's still time. His twenty-two years on the planet have been spent in the United Kingdom, with a few excursions overseas — a particular favourite of his was Amsterdam. Or Norway. Both of which were lovely.

But what Jack lacks in life-experience, he more than makes up for in creative ingenuity. His Jake Tanner series is the birth child of a sinister and twisted mind, and a propensity to assume the worst will happen in even the most mediocre situation.

Finding himself pigeon-holed as a millennial, Jack decided to stick with the stereotype and do things his own way. After all, he felt entitled and he wanted to destroy industries.

Enter: writing.

The love of writing was rekindled in Jack's life when he (briefly) entered the corporate world, and the passion snowballed from there. No more will the millennial writer find himself working 9-5, indulging in the complexities of business life, or wearing a M&S suit.

He will take the world by storm with his pen (keyboard) and his ability to entertain and enthral readers.

Why not join him (and his future dog)?

Keep up to date with Jack at the following:
- Website: https://www.jackprobynbooks.com
- Facebook: https://www.facebook.co.uk/
jackprobynbooks
- Twitter: https://twitter.com/jackprobynbooks
- Instagram: https://www.instagram.com/
jackprobynauthor

Milton Keynes UK
Ingram Content Group UK Ltd.
UKHW041038310723
426072UK00004B/35